I0623584

THE CORRUPTION OF

HANRON

後見

BY
N. K. EDO

PROLOGUE

LONG AGO, BEFORE THE rise of the Kōken, before the cities of men carved paths through the wilderness, there was a forest untouched by time. Its trees stood taller than mountains, their roots winding deep into the earth. It was said that the spirits of the forest spoke to those who listened, offering protection and guidance to travelers and wanderers alike.

But not all who entered the forest sought the wisdom of its spirits. There were those who came with fire in their hands and greed in their hearts, determined to claim the land for themselves. They felled trees and poisoned rivers, seeking to bend nature to their will.

One day, a group of settlers ventured into the forest's heart, driven by hunger and desperation. In their haste, they desecrated a sacred grove, cutting down the ancient trees that had stood for centuries. The spirits, enraged by this violation, began to fade from the land, leaving it defenseless against what was to come.

THE LEGEND OF HANRON

In the place of the fallen trees, something dark began to stir. The settlers spoke of a presence—a shadow that moved between the trees, watching them, waiting. They felt the air grow thick, the ground trembling beneath their feet. Soon, the forest itself turned against them.

From the ashes of that grove, a new force emerged. Hanron, a creature born of contradiction, of twisted nature and corrupted spirits, of life in death, took shape. His body was a shifting mass of sinewy limbs, his eyes an empty void that emanated a low, droning hum. The forest, once a place of balance, became a reflection of Hanron's chaotic essence. Trees twisted into unnatural shapes, animals turned vicious, and his presence corrupted spirits that once protected the land.

The settlers tried to flee, but the forest betrayed them. Paths that had once been safe became mazes of confusion, and those who ventured too far were never seen again. It was said that Hanron moved through the shadows, watching, waiting. His very presence warped the land around him, making the air thick and the ground unstable.

Then, just as quickly as it had begun, the corruption faded. The forest returned to its natural state. The surviving settlers left the area, vowing never to return. The land became known as cursed, and over time, the legend of Hanron became just another story told to scare children.

But the whispers persisted. Over the years, it was said that Hanron would randomly appear in forests far from where he had first emerged, his corruption taking root once again. The trees would twist, the animals would turn, and the air would grow thick with dread. Yet as time passed, these occurrences grew more seldom, until eventually, Hanron was all but forgotten.

1

THE GORGE STRETCHED WIDE, a yawning scar in the belly of the mountains. Steep cliffs rose on either side, their faces worn smooth by centuries of wind and water. Far below, a river wound its way through the depths, glistening faintly in the patches of sunlight that managed to pierce the thick canopy of trees above. The air was cool and still, heavy with the scent of moss and damp earth. No roads led here, no paths carved through the forest. It was a place forgotten by men, hidden from the world.

At the end of the gorge, in a small, tucked-away clearing, stood an old man. His robes were simple and worn, the color of stone and soil, blending him seamlessly into the landscape. He moved slowly, deliberately, his hands working the earth of a small garden nestled in the heart of the clearing. Herbs, carefully cultivated over the years, grew in neat rows, their leaves rustling gently in the faint breeze. The old man, Kaida, bent down, his gnarled fingers lightly brushing over the delicate green stems.

The clearing was quiet but alive with the subtle sounds of nature—a bird's song, the soft rustle of leaves in the wind, the distant murmur of the river far below. Kaida's movements were rhythmic, each pull of a weed or snip of a plant done with the calm precision of a man who had spent years in solitude, tending to the land, listening to the earth breathe.

He plucked a sprig from the soil and paused. The quiet felt different now—too still. He straightened slowly, his brow furrowing as he looked around. The birds had stopped singing, the wind had stilled. Even the rustling of the trees seemed to have quieted, as if nature itself was holding its breath.

Kaida's fingers tightened around the herb as a faint tremor ran through him—not fear, but something more, something deeper. His breath slowed, and his senses reached out, attuned to the slightest shift in the world around him. For a moment, there was nothing—just the stillness of the clearing, the peaceful hum of the earth.

Then he felt it.

A pulse. Faint, distant, but unmistakable. Like a ripple spreading through water, it reached him, carrying with it a sense of unease. The earth beneath his feet felt wrong—no, not here, but far away. Somewhere distant, something stirred. The herb in his hand trembled, and his vision clouded.

In his mind's eye, he saw a forest. Its trees were ancient, their trunks thick with age, but they were no longer whole. The bark split and blackened, the leaves withered and fell, and the ground cracked beneath the weight of something unseen. Dark vines twisted through the roots, creeping across the land like a sickness, spreading, devouring. He saw animals—deer, birds—fleeing, their forms already twisted and wrong.

Kaida's eyes narrowed as the vision shifted. He glimpsed figures—faint, indistinct—moving through the trees. Spirits, perhaps, but not as they should be. The corruption had reached them, too.

He blinked, and the vision shattered, leaving him standing alone in his garden, the sprig still clutched in his hand. The clearing was quiet once more, but the air felt heavy, thick with something unseen.

Kaida crouched for a moment longer, his mind far from the tranquil garden. His voice, low and rough, slipped from his lips as though he were speaking not to himself, but to the earth beneath him.

"Hmm…" He rubbed the leaves between his fingers, feeling their brittleness, their sickness, as if they carried the taint of what he had seen. "The leaves whisper of sickness… but the roots… the roots know more. Always deeper, always quieter." His voice trailed off into a murmur, and his gaze turned toward the ground, as if seeking the truth hidden in the soil itself.

Slowly and with the help of his cane, Kaida rose to his feet, each movement deliberate, as though the weight of the vision clung to his old bones. His back straightened with effort, but his mind remained sharp, keen to the subtle shifts in the world around him. His eyes, though clouded with age, scanned the treetops above, narrowing as he observed the stillness. Even the birds had quieted, the wind hanging heavy and unmoving, as if nature itself was holding its breath.

"Distant," he muttered, his lips barely moving, "but not far enough."

Kaida's eyes glinted with a sharpness that defied his years, searching the sky as though expecting it to tremble under the weight of what was to come. His gaze dropped to the garden, lingering on the small plot of land that had been his refuge for so many years. Here, in this secluded gorge, he had found peace—solace in the solitude of nature's rhythm. But today, the harmony was broken, disturbed by something greater, something darker.

"Something pulls," he continued, wiping the remnants of dirt from his hands onto the rough fabric of his robe. "Tugging at the roots... at the earth itself. It's been waiting, but now..." His words faded again as his thoughts drifted inward, contemplating the ancient forces at play.

There was no hesitation in his movements now, only the certainty that what he had felt could not be ignored. Whatever corruption had taken root in the vision, it was spreading—slowly, quietly—but spreading all the same. The land itself was telling him what no voice could.

Kaida's fingers brushed over the herbs in his garden, his touch reverent but quick. He took one last look around the small clearing, letting his eyes trace the familiar lines of his sanctuary. Here, for so many years, he had tended to nature, nurtured its growth, and in return, it had nurtured him. But this was no time for peace, no time for stillness. His connection to the world around him was too deep, too powerful, to ignore the signs.

"It stirs," he whispered, almost to himself, his voice carrying a weight of ancient understanding. "And it waits... always waiting. For what?"

Kaida's gaze hardened as he turned toward the mouth of the gorge. The path ahead wound through jagged rocks and steep cliffs, a narrow way carved by time and the elements. It was a treacherous route, one that few knew of, and even fewer dared to walk. But for Kaida, it was a familiar journey—one he had made many times in his long life.

The gorge stretched before him like an invitation, its depths shrouded in shadow, the air growing cooler as he approached. He could feel the pull of the distant corruption, calling to him from far beyond the mountains, and his steps quickened with purpose. The peace of his garden was already a memory, fading with each stride he took.

He paused for a moment at the edge of the clearing, glancing back at the sanctuary he had tended for so many years. The small garden, the trees, the earth—it was all part of him, and he had become part of it. But even this place, so far removed from the world, would not remain untouched if the corruption spread. It was all connected, bound by the same breath of life that now trembled with unease.

"Waiting... waiting no longer," Kaida murmured, his voice lost in the wind that had begun to stir once more.

With a final breath, he turned away from the garden and began his descent along the narrow path into the gorge, leaving the safety of his secluded world behind. The sound of the river below grew louder as he walked, the mountains closing in around him like silent sentinels. The path ahead was steep and winding, but Kaida's steps were sure, his resolve unshaken.

He was heading toward the source of the disturbance, the place where the roots of the earth trembled.

THE BUILDING WAS UNUSUALLY quiet, its hallways empty, and the usual hum of activity was absent. Sunlight filtered through the tall, narrow windows, casting long shadows across the polished wooden floors. The only sound was the soft rustling of parchment as Wakamono sat in the main room, poring over an ancient scroll. The room smelled of ink and dust, of knowledge long preserved but rarely disturbed. The quiet felt heavy, a stillness that pressed against his thoughts as he read.

His mind wandered as he stared at the faded characters. The scroll chronicled the early days of the Kōken, warriors who had faced unspeakable horrors to protect the land. Tales of bravery, of sacrifices made, and victories hard-won were etched into the fragile parchment. The Kōken of the past were larger than life, their deeds recorded like legends. But despite the tales of their triumphs, Wakamono couldn't shake the lingering doubts that had taken root since the battle with Onkai.

That fight had been nothing like what he had imagined. Onkai, the massive, hulking akuma, had been terror incarnate—his charred scales impervious to nearly every strike. Wakamono remembered the crushing weight of Onkai's hand, how it had burned through his skin, leaving marks that still hadn't fully healed. His katana had been useless against the akuma's armored hide, and for a moment, Wakamono had felt helpless, trapped in a nightmare where nothing he did mattered.

It wasn't skill or wisdom that had turned the tide. In the heat of the battle, Wakamono had gotten lucky—striking out with the healing blade in a desperate attempt to free himself. The blade had done something neither he nor Red Mist had expected—it had healed a patch of Onkai's charred flesh, leaving it vulnerable to attack. It was pure chance that the blade had landed where it did, but they had both acted quickly, taking advantage of the moment.

Together, as a team, they had defeated the akuma. But the victory didn't feel like a triumph to Wakamono. It felt like a narrow escape, a reminder of how fragile the line between success and failure truly was.

He let out a slow breath, leaning back slightly as his gaze drifted from the scroll. The Kōken of old seemed like untouchable figures—warriors who had stood tall in the face of overwhelming darkness, always knowing the right path, the right decisions. But Wakamono wasn't sure if he had lived up to those ideals. The ancient scrolls didn't tell stories of hesitation, of doubt, of barely scraping by in the face of certain death.

He glanced down at his hands, the faint scars from Onkai's burns still etched into his skin. The healing blade had saved them both, but it hadn't answered the questions gnawing at him.

Had he hesitated too much? Could he have done more? Was he really ready for this life, for the responsibility that came with being a Kōken?

These thoughts had followed him ever since the battle. Red Mist had been right there with him, fighting as his equal, as his guide. She had been the one to read the situation, to exploit the opening he had created. But even in that shared victory, Wakamono couldn't silence the doubts that whispered at the back of his mind.

He thought of the farm he had left behind—his family, his brothers and sister. He had abandoned them to become something greater, something more than just a farmer. But here, sitting in the stillness of the Kōken building, Wakamono wondered if he had truly become that.

The silence pressed in, broken only by the soft rustle of the ancient scroll. He wanted to believe that he was following the right path, but the doubt remained, a quiet weight in his chest that he hadn't yet learned how to bear.

The soft sound of footsteps broke the silence, and Red Mist entered the room. Her presence filled the space, her dark hair tied back, and her face as impassive as ever. She moved with quiet purpose, always in control, always focused on the next task, the next mission. Wakamono glanced up as she approached, carefully folding the scroll he had been reading, though he could still feel the weight of its words pressing on his thoughts.

"Still reading?" she asked, her voice calm and measured. There was no judgment in her tone, only quiet observation. She looked at the scroll in his hands, her sharp eyes taking in the ancient text before settling on him. "It's good to study, but answers will come from experience."

Wakamono's brow furrowed slightly. A part of him felt relief at her words, but another part—the part that had spent the last hour questioning himself—still felt uneasy. "I thought maybe I could learn something more," he said slowly, his voice tinged with frustration. "I didn't do enough against Onkai. I—" He hesitated, searching for the right words. "I keep thinking there's something I missed, something I should have done better."

Red Mist's gaze softened, though her expression remained stoic. She uncrossed her arms and stepped closer, her presence steady and reassuring. "You didn't lack for knowledge, Wakamono," she said, her voice even. "What you lack is experience. That will come in time, with each battle, each challenge."

Wakamono looked down at the scroll in his lap, tracing the faded ink with his fingers. "But the Kōken of the past—"

"—are stories," Red Mist interrupted gently, sitting beside him. "They're based on truth, but they've been shaped, refined. The legends leave out hesitation, fear, doubt—anything that makes the hero seem... human."

She glanced at the scroll, a faint smirk tugging at the corner of her mouth. "Real battles aren't always clean victories, Wakamono. Those Kōken? They didn't win every fight the way these stories say. Some of them barely survived, like we did."

Wakamono met her gaze, her words sinking in. "But the way they're written... it makes it seem like they always knew what to do."

"They didn't always know, but they learned," Red Mist replied. "Just like you're learning now. The battlefield teaches what no scroll can. Mistakes, hesitation... those are part of the journey."

She leaned back slightly, her expression becoming more serious. "We all struggle at first. Every Kōken has moments of doubt, moments where they feel like they've failed. The difference is that they kept going. You've already proven you can adapt in the heat of battle. That's more valuable than anything you'll find in these old stories."

Wakamono felt the tension in his chest begin to ease, though the doubt still lingered. He had survived the battle with Onkai, but that didn't erase the moments of helplessness, the fear that had gripped him in the akuma's grasp. "So, you're saying the legends aren't... real?"

"They're real," Red Mist said. "But they're not the whole truth. What matters is what you learn from them and how you carry that into the next battle." She gave him a firm look. "You adapted. You found a way when there didn't seem to be one. And you did that with me, as a team."

Wakamono nodded slowly, feeling the weight of her words settle. "But it's still not enough. I don't feel like... like I'm ready for what's next."

Red Mist stood and placed a hand on his shoulder, her grip firm and reassuring. "You'll never feel ready," she said. "That's the secret. We face the unknown every time we step out into the world. No amount of training or reading will ever make you feel like you're completely prepared."

Her words, calm and unwavering, gave Wakamono a moment of peace, a quiet assurance that he wasn't as lost as he thought. He still had much to learn, but perhaps that was the path of every Kōken—to grow, to face doubts, and to push forward regardless.

Red Mist's hand lingered on his shoulder for a moment before she stepped back, her eyes now focused on the next task ahead. "You'll have plenty of time to reflect," she said. "But right now, we have work to do."

Before Wakamono could reply, the sharp sound of the door slamming open echoed through the quiet hall, breaking the moment. Both Wakamono and Red Mist turned toward the entrance, their hands instinctively moving to the hilts of their katanas. The sudden noise shattered the calm, and Wakamono's pulse quickened.

A figure stumbled inside, barely able to hold herself upright—Bi.

She was unrecognizable at first, her clothes caked in mud and torn from what had clearly been a perilous journey. Strands of her usually neat, dark hair stuck to her face, damp with sweat and grime. Her breathing came in ragged gasps, each step labored as though her legs could barely carry her weight. Despite her disheveled state, the fire in her eyes hadn't dimmed—she was strong-willed, determined, pushing herself forward even though her body was near its breaking point.

Wakamono's heart leapt into his throat as he recognized her. "Bi!" he called, rushing toward her as she staggered further into the room, her gaze locked onto him, filled with desperation and exhaustion.

She barely managed a weak smile, the relief of seeing her brother evident even through her weariness. But there was something else in her eyes—fear.

"Waka…" she gasped, her voice hoarse and strained. She took another shaky step, her knees nearly giving out beneath her. "It's the farm…" Her voice cracked as she tried to catch her breath, her chest heaving from exertion. "It's… bad."

Her legs buckled, and Wakamono lunged forward, catching her just before she collapsed to the floor. Her weight felt heavier than he remembered—her body weakened, trembling from the arduous journey. He could feel her exhaustion, her vulnerability, but even as he held her, he could see that she was still fighting to stay conscious, fighting to deliver her message.

Bi gripped Wakamono's arm, her fingers cold and shaking, her breaths shallow. "The farm… the forest…" she tried to speak, but the words were barely coherent, fading into quiet gasps as she struggled to stay upright.

"Rest," Red Mist said, stepping closer, her voice calm but sharp with concern. Her eyes swept over Bi, assessing the damage, and Wakamono could sense the urgency building in her. "Tell us everything when you've caught your breath."

Bi nodded weakly, her head slumping against Wakamono's chest as her strength finally gave way. She had fought so hard to reach them, and now, in the safety of her younger brother's arms, her body was demanding rest. Wakamono guided her to a nearby bench, lowering her gently as she leaned heavily against him, her breath still coming in ragged bursts.

Wakamono's mind raced. Whatever had driven Bi to such lengths to reach him, he could only imagine. The farm. Their family.

He exchanged a tense glance with Red Mist, who had already taken a step toward the door, ready for anyone—or anything—that might have followed Bi. Whatever was happening, they could both feel that this was just the beginning.

The quiet dread settled over them again, heavier than before.

3
三

THE ROOM WAS STILL, the cool autumn air seeping in through the cracked window, bringing with it the scent of damp earth and fallen leaves. It contrasted sharply with the heat radiating from Bi's exhausted frame. Wakamono knelt beside her, his brow furrowed with concern. He didn't need to ask; he could see that whatever had driven her here was more than just a simple problem at the farm.

Red Mist, silent as ever, moved quietly to the corner where a pitcher of water sat on a small table. She filled a cup and brought it to Bi without a word, her movements precise but gentle. She set the cup in front of Bi, who accepted it with both hands, though they trembled as she tried to bring it to her lips.

"Drink slowly," Red Mist said, her voice calm but commanding. Bi nodded and took a careful sip, the water cooling her parched throat. Her shoulders, which had been rigid with tension, began to sag slightly as she drank, though Wakamono could still see the tightness in her jaw.

Bi lowered the cup after a few sips, resting it in her lap as she exhaled shakily. Her dark hair, usually tied neatly behind her head, was matted with sweat and dirt, stray strands clinging to her face. She swiped at her forehead with the back of her hand, smearing the dirt further but seeming not to care. Her eyes, though weary, locked onto Wakamono's, and for a brief moment, her lips quirked into a weak smile—an attempt to reassure him, though he could see the fear hiding behind it.

"I'm sorry," she began, her voice hoarse from strain, "I came as fast as I could... but it's bad, Waka."

Wakamono didn't speak. He could feel the weight of her words even before she fully explained. He waited, giving her the space she needed to collect herself.

Bi set the cup down beside her, rubbing her hands together as if to warm them. "It started a few days ago... strange things happening at the farm. The animals... they've gone wild. At first, we thought maybe it was just the cooler weather," she said, her voice faltering. "But it's not that. It's something else. Something... wrong."

Wakamono glanced at Red Mist, whose expression had hardened. She remained still, her eyes focused on Bi, listening intently but saying nothing.

Bi continued, her voice growing quieter. "The crops are dying, too. Overnight. One day they were fine, and the next, it's like they were never alive at all. Everything feels... different. Like the land itself is turning against us."

Wakamono placed a steadying hand on her shoulder. "You did the right thing coming here," he said softly, his tone laced with concern. "You're safe now."

Bi nodded, though the weight of her journey still hung heavy on her shoulders. She took another deep breath, gathering herself before continuing. "Waka... it's not just the farm. It's the whole forest."

Bi drew in a shaky breath, her hands resting in her lap, fingers still trembling slightly. Her voice was quieter now, more reflective, as she began to tell them what had happened.

"It didn't start all at once," she said, her gaze distant as if reliving the events in her mind. "At first, it was subtle—small things that seemed off but easy to ignore. The animals were the first to act strange. Our horses started spooking at shadows, refusing to leave their stables, even when nothing was out of the ordinary." She paused, biting her lip. "We thought it was the change in weather. The days getting shorter, the cold coming in early."

Bi shook her head, frowning. "But then... it got worse. The chickens started attacking each other, pecking until they bled. The cows kicked at anyone who came close, almost like they were being provoked, but there was nothing there. They weren't just scared—they were violent. Aggressive. It was like something had taken hold of them."

Wakamono leaned in, his brow furrowing as he listened closely. He knew Bi wasn't one to panic easily, but the way her voice wavered now sent a chill through him.

"And then the crops," Bi continued, her voice growing quieter. "One morning, they were fine—healthy, ready for harvest. By nightfall, everything had withered. The corn stalks, the rice... all of it. The fields looked like they hadn't been touched by rain in months, but it had only been hours." She rubbed her arms as if trying to shake off the memory. "It didn't make sense."

Wakamono clenched his fists, feeling a knot of worry tighten in his chest. The farm... their home. The thought of it decaying, falling apart, while his family struggled to make sense of the changes filled him with a sense of dread.

Bi continued, her voice strained. "We didn't know what to do. Hokori... he's been trying to keep everyone calm, but even he doesn't understand what's happening." She looked up at Wakamono, her eyes full of concern. "I knew I had to come find you. Whatever this is... it's beyond anything we've ever seen."

She paused again, staring at the floor, and for a moment, the room was silent except for the faint rustling of leaves outside the window. Then, with a deep breath, Bi began to speak again—this time, her voice darker, filled with the memory of her journey.

"I left the farm the next day," she said quietly. "I thought if I got to Sanpuku quickly, I could bring help before things got worse. But the further I traveled, the more... off everything felt."

Her eyes shifted to the window, as if searching for the shadows she had left behind. "It started with the trees," she murmured. "At night, they seemed to move. Not in the wind, but... like they were alive. Watching me. I kept telling myself it was my imagination, that I was just tired, but..." She trailed off, shivering slightly at the memory.

Wakamono leaned closer, his concern deepening. "What happened, Bi?"

She swallowed hard before continuing. "The ani mals... they were different too. There weren't many left, but the ones I saw... they weren't right. Their eyes were wrong. Hollow, glowing. One night, I was walking and I saw a deer standing in the middle of the path." Her voice grew quieter. "Its eyes... they were yellow, glowing like embers. It just stood there, staring at me."

She clenched her hands together, her knuckles white. "I tried to walk around it, but it followed me. I don't know how long it trailed behind me, but it never blinked, never made a sound. Just... watched."

The tension in the room thickened, and Wakamono exchanged a glance with Red Mist. Both of them listened in silence, waiting for Bi to continue.

"The worst was right before I reached the city," Bi said, her voice barely above a whisper now. "There was this buck. Huge, standing in the middle of the road. Its antlers were twisted, gnarled like tree branches, and its eyes were glowing. It charged at me." She shuddered, gripping the edge of the bench tightly. "I barely got out of the way. I had to throw myself down a hill... I spent the night in the dirt, hiding. It was gone by morning, but I didn't feel safe. Not until I reached the city walls."

Her words hung heavy in the air, and for a moment, no one spoke. Wakamono could see the fear still lingering in her eyes, the toll the journey had taken on her spirit. What she had faced had clearly shaken her.

"You've done enough, Bi," Wakamono said softly, placing a hand on her shoulder, trying to offer some comfort. "You're safe now. We'll take care of it."

Bi nodded weakly, though her face was still tight with worry. "But the farm... your brothers..."

"We'll help them," Wakamono assured her. "You've done more than enough already. Rest now."

Bi hesitated, then gave a small, reluctant nod. She leaned back against the wall, her exhaustion finally overtaking her as her eyes fluttered shut. Wakamono stood by her side, watching her breathe slowly, the tension in her body beginning to ease as she drifted into sleep.

Bi's breathing had steadied, her body finally relaxing as sleep took hold. Wakamono watched her for a moment longer, the lines of worry on her face now softened by rest. He let out a slow breath, the weight of her journey settling onto him like a stone in his chest. His mind churned with thoughts of the farm, of Hokori and Baka, and of the strange and sinister changes that had swept through their land.

Red Mist stood by the window, her gaze fixed on the darkening sky outside. The room was silent except for the soft rustle of leaves in the wind and Bi's slow, steady breaths. Wakamono walked over to join her, his eyes still clouded with concern.

"She's exhausted," he said quietly.

Red Mist nodded, her expression as unreadable as ever. "She's strong," she said, though there was an edge to her voice that Wakamono couldn't quite place. "But this... whatever it is... they need our help."

Wakamono frowned, his brow furrowing as he glanced toward his sleeping sister. "Do you think it's like Onkai? Another akuma?"

Red Mist didn't answer immediately. Her eyes remained fixed on the distant horizon, her thoughts clearly racing behind her calm exterior. After a moment, she turned to him, her sharp gaze cutting through the uncertainty that hung between them.

"I don't know," she admitted, her tone clipped. "But something is wrong. Bi's story... the animals, the land itself turning against them—it's not natural." She paused, her hand drifting toward the hilt of her katana. "And it's not just the farm. I can feel it. Whatever's causing this, it's moving, spreading."

Wakamono clenched his fists, his mind replaying Bi's words—the twisted antlers, the glowing eyes, the creeping sense of being watched. His home, the home of so many peaceful farming families, was in danger, and the fear gnawed at him like a constant itch beneath his skin.

"We'll leave as soon as she's strong enough," he said, his voice low but resolute. "We have to protect them. The farm, Hokori, Baka—"

"And the village," Red Mist added. "It won't stop at your family's doorstep. If we don't act quickly, it may consume everything in its path. We don't know the potential breadth of this terror."

Wakamono nodded, though his chest tightened at the thought of facing another unknown threat. Onkai had nearly destroyed them, and though they had come out victorious, the battle had left scars—both on his body and his spirit. The weight of what lay ahead was almost too much to bear, but Red Mist's presence beside him anchored him.

She turned to face him fully, her expression firm but not unkind. "Be ready for anything," she said. "Whatever we're about to face... it won't be like before."

Wakamono swallowed, his jaw tightening as he nodded in agreement. The unease in the air was palpable, and though they had faced great dangers before, something about this felt different. Worse. But he wouldn't let fear paralyze him. Not again.

As they stood there, side by side, the shadows of the coming battle seemed to close in around them. Wakamono cast one last glance at Bi, her form finally at rest, before turning his attention to preparations.

THE SOFT GRAY LIGHT of pre-dawn seeped into the Kōken building, casting the room in muted tones. Outside, the world was still quiet, but the air felt heavy with the promise of action. Red Mist stood by the open door, her eyes fixed on the distant horizon, where the first streaks of light were beginning to break the darkness. She was ready, her katana secured at her side, her posture calm and composed as ever.

Wakamono sat nearby, a scroll of ancient Kōken history unrolled before him, though his eyes weren't focused on the faded ink. His thoughts had already drifted far from the city of Sanpuku—toward the farming settlement, toward the home he had left behind.

The farm. His brothers.

He exhaled slowly, knowing that returning to the farm would stir old tensions. But those thoughts could not take precedence now. Whatever unresolved feelings lingered between him and Hokori, his duty as a

Kōken came first. Protect the farm. Protect the village. That was his mission now.

Red Mist broke the silence, her voice steady and decisive. "We leave at dawn."

There was no hesitation, no room for debate. Wakamono didn't need to question her decision. Their duty was clear: protect those in need, wherever they were. The danger in Sanpuku had subsided, and now they were needed elsewhere.

"The farming settlement is at risk," she continued, still gazing out at the horizon. "It's not just your family, but the entire village. If the corruption spreads, it will destroy everything."

Wakamono nodded, his mind shifting fully to the mission. His brothers, his family, the other villagers—they were all part of the same goal now. "I understand," he said, his voice calm. "We'll protect them."

Red Mist glanced over at him, her sharp gaze studying his face. "There's more at stake here than just the farm. You've seen what happens when we face something like this."

Wakamono met her gaze. The memory of their recent battle against Onkai flashed briefly in his mind—the destruction, the suffering. They had fought for every inch of ground, barely surviving the akuma's relentless onslaught. They had pushed through, relying on their training, their instincts.

But this time, it was different. This time, it wasn't just Sanpuku City. It wasn't just faceless strangers. The village, his family—the people he had known his entire life—were in danger. And the weight of that responsibility settled heavily on his shoulders.

"We won't fail," he said, his voice steady but carrying the weight of the duty ahead. His hands tightened slightly at his sides, as if readying himself for the challenges to come.

Red Mist gave him a single nod, her eyes steady. "Focus on what's in front of you. The rest will come."

Wakamono nodded in return, feeling a sense of resolve solidify within him. "We'll be ready," he said quietly, more to himself than to her.

Red Mist turned back toward the door, the first rays of dawn now casting a faint glow across the landscape outside. "Be ready for anything," she said, her eyes fixed on the horizon.

The dawn was coming, and with it, their mission awaited.

後見

The city was just beginning to wake as Wakamono and Bi walked side by side through the quiet streets. The air was cool, the sky painted in soft shades of pink and orange as the first light of dawn crept over the horizon. Wakamono led the way, his steps steady but deliberate.

Bi glanced around, taking in the unfamiliar sights of Sanpuku. "It's so different here," she murmured, her voice still carrying the weariness from her journey. "I didn't expect it to feel so... distant. Like I'm in a different world completely."

Wakamono smiled faintly, though his thoughts were elsewhere. "It's quieter now than usual."

Bi nodded, but her mind was already drifting back to the farm, to the trouble that awaited them there. "Are we leaving soon?"

Wakamono didn't answer immediately, his eyes fixed on the path ahead. They turned down a narrow street, the buildings casting long shadows in the early morning light. Bi looked at him, waiting for a response, but Wakamono's expression was unreadable.

After a few more moments of walking in silence, Bi frowned. "Where are we going?"

"Just for a walk," Wakamono said, his tone casual. "I mean, you'll see when we get there."

Bi gave him a sideways glance, suspicion creeping into her voice. "Just a walk? Waka?"

Wakamono hesitated, then let out a quiet sigh. He knew Bi wouldn't like this. "We're going to see Mr. and Mrs. Jin."

Bi stopped in her tracks, her eyes narrowing as she turned to face him. "Who? Why?"

Wakamono stopped too, meeting her gaze. "They're good people. I trust them. And I want you to stay with them while we take care of things at home."

Bi's expression hardened, her hands balling into fists at her sides. "Stay with them? What are you talking about? I'm coming with you."

"No, you're not," Wakamono said softly but firmly.

Bi took a step forward, her eyes flashing with anger. "Waka, I'm not a child! I'm not going to just sit here while you go off and—"

"I need you to be safe," Wakamono interrupted, his voice steady despite her rising frustration. "This isn't just about you or me. It's about the whole village, the people there, maybe more. I can't focus on what I need to do if I'm worried about you being in danger."

Bi stared at him, her chest rising and falling with barely contained anger. "So you want me to just... hide away?"

"It's not hiding," Wakamono insisted, his voice gentle but unyielding. "It's being smart. The farm is dangerous, Bi. The village is in danger. You don't know what we're up against."

"And you do?" she shot back, her voice trembling with frustration.

Wakamono shook his head. "No. But I know enough to say that it's not a place for you right now. I need to know you're safe. And I can trust the Jin family to make sure of that."

Bi's fists clenched at her sides, but she didn't speak. The anger in her eyes slowly faded, replaced by something softer—something closer to understanding, though she still hated the idea of being left behind.

"You're really serious about this," she said quietly, her voice losing its sharp edge.

Wakamono nodded. "I am. I wouldn't ask this if I didn't think it was the best thing for you."

They stood in silence for a moment, the tension slowly dissolving between them. Bi let out a sigh, her shoulders slumping slightly in reluctant acceptance.

"Fine," she muttered. "But you better come back."

Wakamono smiled faintly, his eyes softening. "I will."

後見

The morning sun was rising higher in the sky as Wakamono returned to the Kōken building, his mind still on the conversation he'd just had with Bi. The quiet streets of Sanpuku began to stir with life, but for Wakamono, there was no time to focus on the mundane activities of the city. His mission lay elsewhere, and every moment felt like a step closer to danger.

Inside, Red Mist was already making her final preparations. She stood near the armor racks, her movements precise and methodical as she strapped on her light armor. Made of dark, reinforced leather, the armor was designed for mobility as much as protection, allowing for swift movement in battle while still shielding vital areas. The dark material gleamed faintly in the morning light, its intricate details revealing the craftsmanship that had gone into its creation.

Wakamono moved to the adjacent rack and began putting on his own set of armor. His was similar to Red Mist's, though the fit was a bit looser, still adjusting to his frame. The armor felt familiar now, like a second skin—something that had once felt foreign but now served as a reminder of the responsibility he carried.

As he fastened the final straps, Wakamono glanced toward the weapons laid out on the table. His gaze lingered on the katana that had been his companion since the start of his journey. The blade gleamed in the soft light, its sharp edge a testament to the training and discipline he had undergone. Next to it was his wakizashi, a shorter blade that complemented his katana, useful in close combat and more confined spaces.

Red Mist was checking her own weapons—a finely crafted katana with a lacquered sheath, its hilt wrapped in red silk. She also carried a tanto, a small dagger strapped to her waist, and a set of kunai knives tucked discreetly into her belt. Every tool had its place, and Red Mist wielded each with a precision that came from years of experience.

But it was the healing blade that drew Wakamono's attention most. The broken katana lay in its sheath, strapped to his back. Though it had been the key to their victory over Onkai, today it again felt like an enigma—an ancient relic with a purpose they didn't fully understand. Its power had saved them once, but Wakamono had learned not to rely on it too heavily. It was there if needed, but this time, the fight would be different.

Red Mist glanced over at him as she tightened the final strap on her armor. "Ready?"

Wakamono nodded, fastening the healing blade securely across his back. He strapped his katana to his side and checked the weight of his wakizashi. "Ready."

Red Mist didn't speak further, but her eyes conveyed all that needed to be said. The task ahead was dangerous, and there was no room for doubt or hesitation. Wakamono could see the calm resolve in her posture, a steadiness that he had come to rely on.

Without another word, they stepped out of the building and into the street. The city stretched out before them, but their destination lay beyond the city walls—toward the farm, toward the forest that now held an unknown threat. As they walked, Wakamono felt the weight of his weapons at his side, a familiar but sobering sensation.

Every step brought them closer to the danger that awaited, but Wakamono's resolve was set. His thoughts were clear—protect the village, protect the farm, and do what was necessary to stop the spreading corruption.

The journey had begun.

5

THE AIR IN THE forest had changed. Kaida could feel it—thick and heavy, like a brewing storm that hadn't yet broken. The vibrant green of the leaves had dulled to a sickly hue, and the once-healthy trees seemed to droop, as though weighed down by an unseen burden. The old seer paused on the narrow path, his sharp eyes scanning the canopy above, his senses attuned to the wrongness in the air.

He had walked these woods many times, and though the passage of years had slowed his steps, nothing could dull his connection to the world around him. The breeze carried whispers—echoes of the forest's distress, though the wind itself was still.

Kaida's path led him deeper into the forest, his gnarled hand tracing the contours of an ancient staff as he walked. His robes brushed lightly against the undergrowth, a soft rustling that barely disturbed the quiet. But it wasn't long before he saw it—a tree, standing apart from the others, its bark blackened and twisted, its branches brittle, as though scorched by invisible flames.

Kaida stopped in front of the corrupted tree, his eyes narrowing. He extended a hand, palm facing the charred bark. The once-thriving oak was suffocating beneath the weight of some unknown malevolence, and its sickness radiated outward, a stain on the surrounding life.

Slowly, Kaida placed his hand on the tree, feeling the rot beneath his fingers. The bark crumbled slightly at his touch, flakes of blackened wood drifting to the forest floor. His breath came steady as he closed his eyes, reaching out with his spirit to the heart of the tree, searching for the life that remained within.

With a soft murmur, he began, his voice low and measured:

"Beneath bark and root,
Life stirs where darkness once crept,
Hope blossoms again."

As the final words left his lips, a faint glow pulsed beneath his palm. The sickly blackness that marred the tree's surface began to fade, the dark veins retreating into the wood as if chased away by Kaida's words. The brittle branches slowly regained their strength, and new leaves sprouted where dead ones had fallen. The tree stood straighter, its bark smoothing out, a soft green light flickering in the spaces where the decay had once spread.

Kaida withdrew his hand, watching as the tree slowly returned to life, the corruption lifting from it like a shroud being cast aside. The forest around him, though seemingly still, felt disturbed. The natural order was disrupted, tainted by a force far more insidious than a simple sickness. The trees still whispered their warnings, but the words were jumbled, fragmented—unable to convey the full extent of the danger.

And then, a voice.

"So careful, so deliberate..." The voice was soft, lilting, with a strange warmth that didn't match the dark atmosphere. "Do you plan to heal the entire forest, old man? One tree at a time?"

Kaida didn't stiffen at the voice; he had expected something, though he had hoped it wouldn't be her. Instead, he paused, his hand lingering on the tree for a moment longer before he turned.

A woman stepped out from the shadows, her bare feet making no sound on the forest floor. She was beautiful, with smooth, flawless skin and long black hair that cascaded over her shoulders like silk. Her robes were delicate, almost shimmering in the faint light, as though she were a spirit born of the forest itself. Her movements were graceful, fluid, her presence somehow commanding and serene.

But Kaida felt the evil in her immediately. It lingered beneath the surface, just out of sight but palpable. There was an air of cold malice in the way she smiled, a gleam of mockery in her eyes that betrayed her true nature.

"You hide well," Kaida said evenly, his voice calm. "But your mask does not fool me."

The woman's smile widened, her dark eyes glinting with amusement. "Of course not," she said, her tone light and playful. "But isn't it better this way? Don't you miss beauty, Kaida?"

Kaida's hand instinctively brushed the amulet hanging from his neck, but his expression remained impassive. "Yama-uba," he said, naming her plainly. "I only see the corruption beneath your guise."

The playful look in her eyes darkened, though her smile remained. She took a step closer, her movements smooth and deliberate. "It seems your age hasn't dulled your sight after all."

Kaida didn't respond, his fingers still resting lightly on the amulet. Yama-uba's gaze flicked toward the talisman, and her smile twisted into something more sinister.

"Ah, your little trinket," she purred. "It keeps me from crawling inside your mind, doesn't it? Clever. But it won't protect you from what's coming."

Kaida's eyes narrowed slightly, though his voice remained steady. "What is coming?"

Yama-uba's laughter was soft, like the rustling of dead leaves. She circled him slowly, her feet barely making a sound on the earth. "Something far greater than you, old man. Something your little charms can't hold back. The corruption you felt here—it's only a taste."

Kaida watched her with quiet caution. "I've lived long enough to know when evil is creeping," he said. "I've seen your kind before."

Yama-uba stopped, turning to face him fully. Her smile faded slightly, her eyes growing colder. "Have you now?" Her voice dropped, losing some of its playfulness. "This is different, Kaida. This isn't just another passing evil. This is something that will take root. It will spread, and you will watch it consume everything you've spent your life protecting."

Her eyes glinted as she stepped closer, leaning in slightly. "And the boy—the young Kōken—he will fall. Do you really think you can protect him? One tree at a time? Go back to hiding in your cave."

Kaida's hand tightened around his staff, but his expression remained unreadable. "I will do what I must," he said quietly.

Yama-uba's smile returned, though now it was sharper, more mocking. "Of course you will." She began to fade into the mist that seemed to rise from the earth itself. "But you're running out of time, old man. The forest is already lost."

Her voice lingered even after her form had disappeared, like an echo that refused to fade.

THE ROAD OUT OF Sanpuku stretched ahead, a familiar path that wound through the gently sloping farmlands and quiet villages that dotted the landscape. Wakamono and Red Mist moved at a steady pace, their light armor rustling softly with each step, the rhythm of their journey blending with the stillness of the early morning.

The village they approached was a place Wakamono knew well, though it had been some time since he had passed through. It was small, modest, with simple homes and narrow streets. The villagers were just beginning to stir, their morning routines underway as they tended to their animals or prepared for the day's work. Yet something about the atmosphere felt off.

The usual hum of activity was quieter here, the villagers moving about with a sense of purpose but without the usual chatter or greetings exchanged. Wakamono's gaze swept over the familiar scene, his eyes catching on the haunted well at the center of the village square.

He felt a subtle shift in the air, a prickle of awareness creeping along his skin. His memories of this place were clear—this was where it had all begun for him. The first encounter that had shaken his resolve, the first taste of what it meant to be a Kōken. But today, it felt different. He was different.

The well sat untouched, its stone surface covered in a fine layer of dust. The villagers gave it a wide berth, avoiding even glancing in its direction as they went about their tasks. The aura around it was unmistakable, a lingering malevolence that had haunted the village.

Without breaking stride, Wakamono's eyes narrowed as they locked onto the well. He slowed his pace slightly, the tension in the air thickening as they approached. Red Mist walked beside him, her gaze flicking toward him as she sensed the shift in his focus.

"Give me one moment," Wakamono said quietly, his voice calm but firm.

Red Mist nodded as she slowed her pace, allowing him to step ahead.

Wakamono moved toward the well, his steps deliberate. The faintest whisper of scratching reached his ears, the sound so subtle it might have been missed by anyone else. He stopped at the edge of the well, his hand resting lightly on the hilt of his katana, eyes narrowing as he peered into the darkness below.

For a moment, there was silence. Then, with a familiar creaking sound, a skeletal hand emerged from the shadows, its bony fingers grasping at the edge of the well, dragging itself upward. Wakamono didn't hesitate.

In a single, fluid motion, Wakamono drew his katana and slashed downward. The creature's hand was severed instantly, the bones clattering to the ground beside the well before the rest of its body could even surface. Wakamono thrust the blade through the top of the creatures skull, so far that it's shine could be seen behind the bare ribs of the skeleton. He swung up, throwing the beast in an arch over himself before smashing it onto the hard ground. The action was so swift, so precise, that the threat had been neutralized before it could even fully take shape. The bones lay scattered.

Wakamono sheathed his blade without ceremony, his expression calm, as if the entire encounter had been nothing more than a minor inconvenience. He turned away from the well, not bothering to look back at the skeleton that had once been his first true challenge.

Red Mist's eyes lingered on him for a moment, a flicker of approval in her gaze. She said nothing, but the brief nod she gave him spoke volumes. Wakamono had grown since that first encounter. He wasn't the same frightened boy who had stumbled his way to Sanpuku.

"Give these bones a proper burial," Red Mist spoke to a local who had stopped to watch the spectacle, "and the creature will haunt your well no more. Do it today, before the sun sets."

Together, they moved on, the haunted well quickly fading into the background as they continued their journey. The road ahead lay open, but the sense of unease followed them, lingering just beyond sight.

後見

The dense woods stretched before them, the trees towering high above, their branches knitting together to block out much of the light. The air grew heavier, the once-refreshing breeze replaced by a damp, suffocating stillness.

Wakamono glanced around, his hand resting on the hilt of his sword as they walked deeper into the woods. There was something unnatural about the silence here—a stillness that seemed to hold its breath, waiting for something to happen. His instincts screamed that they were being watched, though he could see no one.

"The air feels strange," he murmured, his voice low.

Red Mist nodded slightly but kept her gaze forward. Her hand hovered near her katana as they pressed on. "It's the land itself. It's sick."

And it was. The further they went, the more twisted and unnatural the forest became. The once-healthy trees now bent at odd angles, their bark blackened and split as though something had clawed at them from the inside. Vines coiled around their trunks like serpents, thick and pulsating, as though the forest was slowly being strangled by its own growth.

Patches of the ground were cracked and dry, as if the life had been sucked out of the soil, leaving only brittle remnants behind. In other places, the earth was damp and slick, covered with a foul-smelling sludge that clung to their feet with each step. The forest felt alive but not in the way it should have been. It was as though something dark had taken root here, warping everything it touched.

Wakamono knelt briefly beside a fallen tree, running his hand along its withered bark. It crumbled beneath his fingers, turning to dust with the slightest touch.

"This isn't natural," he said quietly. "The forest is rotting from the inside."

Red Mist gave no reply but remained on high alert, her eyes scanning the surroundings for any further signs of danger. The oppressive silence continued to bear down on them, and Wakamono couldn't shake the feeling that they weren't alone. The corruption wasn't just in the land—it was in the air, in the animals, in everything around them.

As if in answer to his thoughts, they came across a clearing where a small herd of deer stood, grazing on the sparse grass. But something was wrong. Their coats were patchy, their fur falling out in clumps, revealing raw, inflamed skin underneath. Their eyes were dull and glassy, clouded over as if the animals were not fully aware of their surroundings.

One of the deer lifted its head to look at them, its movements slow and unnatural. Its jaws moved mechanically, chewing at nothing, while its legs trembled as though it could barely hold itself upright.

Wakamono's hand tightened on the hilt of his katana, but he didn't draw it. The deer didn't seem to be a threat—just another sign of how deeply the corruption had spread. Still, their vacant stares sent a shiver down his spine.

"They're sick," he whispered. "The forest is making them sick."

Red Mist watched the animals with narrowed eyes. "The corruption isn't just in the land. It's spreading to everything."

They continued deeper into the woods, the twisted shapes of the trees looming over them like skeletal hands reaching out from the darkness. The feeling of being watched never left Wakamono, and every now and then, he would catch a glimpse of movement out of the corner of his eye—something darting between the trees, too quick to see clearly.

A mangy fox crossed their path at one point, its once-bright fur dull and matted with filth. Its eyes were wild, bloodshot, as it watched them pass. There was no fear in the animal, only a cold, unnatural gaze that sent another shiver down Wakamono's spine.

The further they went, the worse it became. Birds with disheveled feathers and broken wings perched on twisted branches, their beady eyes following Wakamono and Red Mist with unnerving focus. The birds didn't move—didn't chirp or caw—just sat there, watching silently as the pair passed beneath them.

Wakamono's chest tightened with unease. Every step felt like it was taking them deeper into something alive—something hostile. The air around them seemed to thrum with a low hum, a vibration that Wakamono could feel in his bones.

Red Mist's hand never left her sword as they pressed on, her gaze fixed on the path ahead. "Whatever this is, it's growing stronger."

Wakamono nodded silently, his mind racing with the possibilities. If the corruption had reached this far, there was no telling what they would find at the farm. His family, the villagers—they were all at the mercy of whatever had taken hold of the forest.

And they were running out of time.

後見

The sun dipped low on the horizon, casting long shadows over the road as Wakamono and Red Mist continued their journey. The forest behind them gave way to open fields, signaling that the farming village was near. The day was fading into evening, and the golden light of the setting sun bathed the landscape in a soft, almost serene glow.

Wakamono's pace slowed slightly as they approached the edge of the farmlands. His mind wandered back to the first time he had made this journey—young, inexperienced, and eager for adventure. Back then, the road had seemed impossibly long, each step taking him further from everything he had known. Now, it felt different. The distance no longer felt daunting, his steps more sure, the weight of his duty as a Kōken grounding him.

It all seemed so much shorter now.

He glanced at the sky, watching the last rays of sunlight slip below the distant hills. It wasn't just the physical distance that had changed—it was him. He had come so far, faced so much, and yet the closer they got to the village, the more unsettled he felt.

But as his thoughts drifted, something gnawed at the edge of his awareness. A sense of unease crept into his mind, subtle at first, like the faintest whisper of unease carried on the breeze.

Ahead of them, the farmland stretched out in quiet rows, the familiar sight of the village just beyond. At first glance, everything seemed as it should—rolling fields of crops, the roofs of homes in the distance, the silhouette of barns against the darkening sky. For a fleeting moment, Wakamono almost allowed himself to believe that nothing had changed.

But as they drew closer, the truth became harder to ignore.

The land, once fertile and vibrant, had been touched by the same corruption they had seen in the forest. It was as if the life had been drained from the earth itself. The crops that should have been standing tall were withered, their stalks bent and broken. The soil, usually rich and dark, was cracked and dry, as though the land had been scorched by an invisible fire. Vines crawled over the remains of the crops, twisted and gnarled, choking whatever life remained. The dried up rice paddies held only thick sludge.

Wakamono's breath caught in his throat as he took in the full extent of the damage. He had expected signs of the corruption, but not like this. The farmland was more devastated than he had imagined, more spoiled than anything they had seen on their journey so far.

Red Mist stopped beside him, her eyes narrowing as she surveyed the landscape. "It's worse than I thought."

Wakamono nodded, his gaze lingering on the nearest field. The crops were beyond saving, their leaves brittle and gray. He could see no movement, no sign of the villagers who should have been working the fields this time of day. The silence hung heavy in the air, broken only by the soft rustle of the wind through the dying crops.

"This is my home," Wakamono said quietly, more to himself than to Red Mist. The sight of the corrupted farmland cut deeper than he expected, a hollow ache settling in his chest. This was the land he had grown up on, the fields he had played in as a child. And now, they were nearly unrecognizable.

Red Mist glanced at him but said nothing. There was nothing to say. The sickness had spread deeper into the heart of the village than they had feared.

"We need to move quickly," Red Mist said, her voice calm but firm. "Whatever did this can't be far."

Wakamono nodded again, his hand instinctively going to the hilt of his katana as they pressed forward. The sense of unease that had been growing within him now bloomed into full awareness. The corruption wasn't just in the land—it was alive, spreading, and it was waiting for them.

They would reach his family farm soon, but as the sun dipped below the horizon and shadows crept across the fields, Wakamono couldn't shake the feeling that they were already too late.

七

THE VILLAGE SEEMED EVEN quieter than the road
leading up to it. Wakamono and Red Mist walked side
by side through the narrow dirt paths, their footsteps
the only steady rhythm in an otherwise still world.
The houses were modest, built from worn wood and
cracked stone, their exteriors showing signs of disre-
pair. Stray dogs barked anxiously in the distance, their
hackles raised as they darted between the shadows of
the buildings.

Wakamono felt the eyes of the villagers on
them—wary glances cast from doorways, some people
huddling together, whispering as they passed. There
was fear in their faces, mixed with something else. It
was the look of people who had seen too much but
didn't know how to ask for help. A few of them offered
polite nods but quickly retreated to their homes, the
doors creaking shut behind them.

Red Mist's expression remained impassive, her
gaze forward, but Wakamono could feel the tension
building in the air. It was thick, heavy with unspoken

fears, the weight of which seemed to grow with every step they took toward his family's farm.

Wakamono's thoughts turned inward as they walked deeper into the village. It had been so long since he had set foot here, and yet the familiarity of the place brought with it a strange sense of discomfort. This was home—his past—but it no longer felt like it. There were many memories here, some buried, others fresh, all of them stirring in him as they approached.

Suddenly, a soft voice broke through the quiet.

"Wakamono?"

Wakamono turned to see an elderly woman stepping forward from one of the nearby homes. Her frail figure moved slowly, her white hair tied back in a loose knot, and her clothes faded from years of wear. She smiled warmly at him, her eyes soft with recognition, though there was a unnerving look to them, as though she were seeing someone else through him.

"My, my... your father knew you'd return one day," she said, her voice gentle, almost wistful. She clasped her hands together in front of her, the wrinkles in her skin deepening as she did. "He always said you'd come back to us."

Wakamono felt his chest tighten at the mention of his father. He forced a respectful smile, bowing his head slightly in greeting. "It's good to see you again," he replied, though his voice lacked the warmth that hers carried.

The old woman's gaze drifted past him for a moment, her eyes distant as though searching for something lost in the fog of her memories. Then she smiled again, but this time there was something sad in it.

"And your mother... such a pretty woman," she murmured, her voice dropping to a whisper. "I remember when she used to walk through these street s... so graceful... so beautiful..."

Wakamono froze, his breath catching in his throat. His mother. The woman who had died the day he was born. How long had it been since she walked these streets, when had she been the woman the elder was recalling? And yet the old woman spoke as if she could still see her, as if her memory lived on in the village in ways that Wakamono had never known.

The words cut deep, stirring something in him he thought had been buried. He knew the woman was delusional, that time had warped her memories, and yet the ache was there, sharp and undeniable.

Red Mist stood quietly beside him, her presence solid and unwavering, but Wakamono could feel the weight of her gaze on him. She said nothing, offering him no comfort—only silent understanding.

Wakamono swallowed hard, pushing the pain down, burying it beneath the surface as he always did. He bowed his head again, his voice steady, though softer now. "Thank you."

The woman blinked, as if startled by his response, and then nodded slowly, her smile returning as she patted his arm with a trembling hand, squeezing gently, though he imagined it was all of her strength. "You've done well to come back, Wakamono. Your father... he must be proud. He will be so happy to see you home."

He forced another smile, though his heart ached. "I hope so."

With that, the old woman turned and shuffled back toward her home, her figure soon disappearing into the shadows of her doorway. The village was quiet once more, though the weight of her words lingered in the air like a heavy mist.

Wakamono exhaled, the tension still coiled tight in his chest. Red Mist looked at him but said nothing. She didn't need to. They both knew there were some things that could never be resolved, some wounds that would never truly heal.

"Let's go," Wakamono said quietly, his voice steady again.

Red Mist nodded, and together they continued toward the farm, leaving the woman—and the ghosts of the past—behind them.

Twilight had settled in fully by the time Wakamono and Red Mist reached the family farm. The familiar fields stretched out in all directions, but they too bore the marks of the corruption. Trees that once lined the edge of the property now leaned ominously, their branches twisted and skeletal. The earth itself seemed lifeless, cracked in places where crops had once thrived. It was home, but it felt alien now, as though something had stolen its soul while Wakamono had been away.

The farmhouse came into view, its weathered wood glowing faintly in the fading light. A familiar smell of smoke from the hearth lingered in the air. Wakamono felt a tightness in his chest—returning here brought back memories of the life he had left behind, but there was no time for reflection.

They approached the door in silence, Red Mist's presence beside him as solid as a stone wall. The soft rustle of the wind through the fields was the only sound, until the door creaked open with a long, drawn-out groan.

Hokori stepped into the doorway, his broad shoulders filling the frame. His face, usually impassive, was tight with something unspoken. His eyes immediately went to Wakamono, scanning him, but the first words out of his mouth weren't a greeting.

"Where is Bi?"

Wakamono nodded his head, his expression calm. "She's safe. I left her in Sanpuku, with the Jins."

Hokori's eyes relaxed, though the stiffness in his posture didn't ease. His jaw clenched as if bracing himself for more, his gaze flicking briefly to Red

Mist before returning to Wakamono. "Good," he said, though the word held little warmth.

There was an awkward pause as Hokori's eyes finally settled on Red Mist, who stood beside Wakamono, her presence commanding despite her quiet demeanor. She observed him with her usual stoic calm, offering nothing more than a nod in greeting.

Wakamono glanced at her and turned to his brother. "This is Red Mist," he said simply. "My mentor."

Hokori's lips pressed into a thin line. He gave a curt nod but said nothing, his gaze lingering on Red Mist a little too long, though he tried to mask his discomfort. He crossed his arms over his chest, as though building a barrier between himself and whatever emotions might surface.

Before the tension could grow thicker, Baka appeared from the dimly lit interior. His face lit up at the sight of Wakamono, his wide grin a stark contrast to Hokori's tight expression.

"Waka! You're back!" Baka rushed forward, his enthusiasm breaking the tension. His broad, childlike smile was genuine, and he clapped Wakamono on the back with a heavy hand. "I knew you'd come."

Wakamono couldn't help but smile, the warmth of his brother's greeting cutting through the coldness in the air. "Of course I would."

Baka's attention quickly shifted to Red Mist, and his wide eyes grew even wider as he stared at her in awe. "So... you're the Red Mist?" he asked, his voice full of wonder. He blinked, clearly captivated by her, as though he were looking at some mythical figure from the stories he had heard over the years.

Red Mist, with her long, dark hair tied back in a simple but practical style, stood tall and calm, her sharp features catching the last of the twilight. Her armor, though light, was intricately detailed, the dark fabric well-worn from years of battle, but it gave her a sense of timeless power. To Baka, she must have looked like the embodiment of the Kōken legends, a warrior standing on the edge of shadow and light.

Baka, still staring, tried to make conversation. "Do you... uh, do you like farming?"

Wakamono shot his brother a sidelong glance, but Red Mist didn't even blink at the question. She merely inclined her head slightly, her expression unchanged. "I respect those who can cultivate life," she said in her calm, measured tone.

Baka, taking her response as encouragement, continued. "We grow some good crops here—well, we used to." His voice faltered as he gestured vaguely toward the fields, where the corruption was painfully evident.

Red Mist's eyes flicked to the farm, her sharp gaze taking in the details—the withered crops, the patches of lifeless earth, the vines that had crept into every corner.

"It's been hard," Baka said, his voice quieter now. "But the land will heal, now that Waka is home."

The tension slowly settled into an uneasy calm as they moved into the house. Hokori lingered at the back, his arms still crossed, his silence louder than any words. His eyes remained fixed on Wakamono, as if waiting for something more, something that might never come.

As they stepped inside, Wakamono felt the weight of the past pressing down on him, heavier than ever. This was his family, his home, but the distance between him and Hokori felt greater than the miles he had traveled to return here. He thought of his father's grisly death and wondered how much Hokori blamed him for it.

Red Mist glanced around the small home, her expression unreadable. She gave no sign of judgment or approval, merely observing the surroundings with her usual cool detachment.

"We'll need to stay alert," she finally said, her voice cutting through the silence like a blade. "The source of the corruption isn't far."

Hokori, still standing in the doorway, nodded grimly. "We know."

The room fell into a strained silence, the weight of the decay outside seeping into the walls of the house, a quiet reminder that danger loomed closer with every passing moment.

8

八

THE FARMHOUSE PORCH CREAKED softly beneath their weight as Wakamono and Baka sat side by side, the cool evening air settling in around them. The sun had long since dipped below the horizon, casting the farm in deep shadow. A few distant stars blinked into existence above, their faint glow barely breaking the thickening dusk. The quiet of the countryside enveloped them, a silence only punctuated by the occasional chirp of insects or the distant rustle of the wind through the trees.

Baka, sitting with his arms loosely resting on his knees, didn't seem to notice the heaviness of the air, nor the subtle tension creeping around them. His wide, boyish grin remained firmly in place as he launched into his usual chatter, his voice cutting through the quiet like an anchor to the everyday life that still existed here, despite everything.

"The chickens, they've been stubborn lately," he said, shaking his head with a small chuckle. "Always running off, getting into the strangest places. You wouldn't believe where I found one the other day—up in the rafters of the barn. Don't know how she got up there, but it took me half the morning to get her down."

Wakamono listened in silence, his gaze drifting out over the darkened fields. His thoughts were elsewhere, his senses quietly alert to the world around him. The farm looked the same as it always had, the familiar landscape of his childhood. But now, there was something off—an almost imperceptible wrongness that he couldn't shake. It was as though the land itself was holding its breath, waiting for something to happen.

Baka, completely unaware of his brother's inner turmoil, continued on, his voice light and untroubled. "And the crops... well, they've been struggling, as you can see." He gestured toward the fields, where the signs of corruption were more evident with each passing day. "But I reckon they'll bounce back. They always do after a tough season."

Wakamono nodded absently, not really hearing the words. His hand rested on the hilt of his katana, a habit he had picked up. There was comfort in the familiar grip of the weapon, a reminder of the battles he had fought, the dangers he had faced. And yet, here, at the farm—his home—he felt more exposed than he had in any battle.

Baka continued to talk, the conversation drifting from one mundane topic to the next. "You know, the door to the shed's been giving me trouble. I keep meaning to fix that hinge. One of these days, I'll get around to it. But you know how it is—there's always something else that needs doing."

Wakamono nodded again, his attention still divided, his senses tuned to the environment around them. The air had grown unnaturally still, the wind having quieted to an almost eerie calm. He could feel it—a shift, subtle but undeniable. Something dark was closing in, pressing against the edges of the peaceful moment.

"I'm glad you're back," Baka said suddenly, breaking the rhythm of his small talk. His voice was softer now, more sincere. "I always knew you'd be back."

Wakamono didn't offer any words of reassurance, just nodded again, acknowledging his brother's sentiment. But even as Baka spoke, that same sense of unease stirred within him. It gnawed at the edges of his awareness, growing stronger with every passing second. The wind had changed, though it was barely noticeable to anyone who wasn't attuned to such things.

Wakamono's hand tightened slightly on his katana, his thumb brushing the edge of the hilt. He could feel the shift in the air—an almost palpable warning that something wasn't right. It was coming. Whatever

69

darkness had settled over the farm, whatever corruption had taken hold, it was moving closer.

He glanced at Baka, who was blissfully unaware, still caught up in his lighthearted stories. Wakamono didn't want to disturb the fragile peace of the moment, but deep inside, he knew it wouldn't last.

Something was coming.

Something was here.

後見

Red Mist sat by the edge of the stream, her eyes closed as she focused on the gentle murmur of the water. It was not a place of familiarity or comfort—just a quiet spot she had found near the farm, where she could clear her mind. The cool air carried the scent of damp earth and distant pine, calming her thoughts. She breathed deeply, her hand resting lightly on the hilt of her katana.

The silence of the evening was peaceful, but it did not lull her into relaxation. She was always ready—her mind and body attuned to the world around her. The soft bubbling of the stream, the whisper of the wind through the trees... it all seemed too quiet now, too still.

Then, she felt it.

A chill crept through the air, faint at first but unmistakable. Her sharp instincts honed over years of training told her something was wrong. Red Mist's eyes opened, her hand tightening around her sword as she slowly scanned the forest.

At first, there was nothing but shadows, stretching and shifting in the fading light. Then, from the darkness, a figure emerged.

Old, hunched, and frail, the figure moved slowly, her gnarled hands barely visible beneath the tattered robes that hung from her thin frame. Her hair, long and white, hung in tangled strands around a wrinkled face, hollow eyes gleaming with malice.

Yama-uba.

The sight of her sent a cold shiver down Red Mist's spine, but she did not flinch. She stood her ground, watching as Yama-uba crept closer, her movements deliberate, as though savoring each step.

"You...," Red Mist murmured, her voice low, more a statement than a question. "What are you doing here?"

Yama-uba didn't answer immediately. Instead, she tilted her head, her lips twisting into a crooked, almost amused smile. She shuffled closer, her feet barely making a sound as they moved over the moss-covered ground.

"The boy," Yama-uba rasped, her voice like the crackle of dry leaves. "He dies."

Red Mist's eyes narrowed, her grip tightening on her katana. "What are you talking about?" she asked, her tone sharp. She didn't let her guard down for a moment, but something in Yama-uba's words struck a chord of unease.

Yama-uba's gaze remained fixed on Red Mist, her eyes gleaming with something dark, something ancient. She took another step closer. "You feel it?" she whispered, her voice barely more than a breath. "The stirring... the shadows... creeping. It's all around you, Chikara."

Red Mist stood tall, her eyes never leaving Yama-uba. "If you've come to threaten him, you're wasting your time. He's becoming a fine warrior."

The old woman's lips curled into a smile, again, but there was no warmth in it—only malice. "Oh, I'm not here to threaten... only to warn." She took another step forward, her presence oppressive now, her frail frame somehow radiating power. "The boy is fragile. And soon, he will fall."

Red Mist clenched her jaw, her muscles tense. "What is happening here?" she demanded, but Yama-uba offered no direct answers. Instead, she took one more step, her bony hand reaching out as if to brush the air near Red Mist.

"It is beginning," Yama-uba whispered, her voice chilling and final.

Red Mist felt the weight of those words settle over her. There was no more time for questions, no more time for cryptic games. She knew what she had to do.

Without another word, she spun on her heel and bolted toward the farmhouse, her movements swift and precise. As she ran, the sound of Yama-uba's laughter echoed behind her, thin and twisted, lingering in the air like a curse.

The forest blurred around her as Red Mist pushed herself harder, the farmhouse coming into view in the distance. And then, the night erupted—screeching birds, wild deer, and flashes of red eyes. Chaos had already descended upon the farm.

後見

Hokori worked in the fields, his strong hands tugging at the dead plants that had once flourished. The brittle stems snapped easily under his grip, their once vibrant green leaves now crumbling to dust. His brow furrowed in frustration as he tossed another handful of withered crops to the ground. Nothing here was the same anymore—not the land, not the air, and certainly not the family.

The last rays of daylight clung to the horizon, casting long shadows over the fields. Hokori muttered under his breath, his thoughts dark and restless. He yanked another dead plant from the soil, the earth dry and cracked beneath it. The weight of the failing farm pressed heavily on his shoulders, a burden he had been forced to carry alone.

A sudden stillness settled over the fields, the evening air growing unnaturally cold. Hokori paused, his hand frozen in the dirt, sensing something wrong. His eyes lifted toward the treeline, where the last light of day barely touched the branches. For a moment, everything was silent—too silent.

And then, it came.

A shrill cry pierced the air, cutting through the stillness like a blade. Hokori whipped his head around just in time to see a dark shape swooping down from the sky. A bird, its wings tattered and broken, eyes glowing an unnatural red, dove toward him with a wild screech. He barely had time to duck before its claws raked the air where his face had been.

Chaos erupted around him. More birds appeared out of the shadows, their wings ragged, their movements erratic. They dived at him from all angles, their beaks sharp and hungry. Hokori swatted at them with his arms, but they were too fast, too vicious. Talons raked over him, drawing blood to stain his ragged shirtsleeves.

From the edges of the field, twisted shapes emerged. Deer, their bodies contorted and unnatural, charged through the crops, their jagged antlers glinting in the fading light. Their movements were jerky, as if their very bones were rebelling against them. They plowed through the brittle plants, their hooves tearing up the earth as they barreled toward Hokori.

He cursed under his breath, stumbling backward, his hands scrambling for anything to defend himself. But before he could react, a flash of white darted out from the shadows—a small rabbit, no larger than any he had seen before. But its eyes burned with a fierce red glow, and its mouth twisted in a snarl showing nasty, big, pointy teeth. The rabbit crouched low for a brief moment, its gaze locking onto Hokori's, before it leapt at him with a ferocity that belied its size.

Hokori barely managed to dodge the creature as it sailed past him, its teeth gnashing the air where his neck had been. He stumbled, falling backward into the dirt, his heart pounding in his chest. The birds continued to dive and claw at him, while the deer trampled closer, their antlers poised to strike.

Back at the farmhouse, Wakamono and Baka shot to their feet as the sound of chaos reached their ears. The night, once quiet and still, had transformed into a cacophony of shrieks and growls. Wakamono's hand flew to his katana, his pulse quickening as he glanced toward the field where Hokori had been working.

Without a word, Wakamono sprinted toward the commotion, his mind racing. Beside him, Baka followed, his face a mask of confusion and fear. The peaceful moment they had been sharing was shattered in an instant, replaced by the raw, immediate need to protect.

As Wakamono neared the edge of the field, the sight before him turned his blood cold. The corrupted animals were everywhere—birds with glowing eyes, their wings tattered and torn, swooped through the air, their shrieks filling the night. Deer, their antlers twisted and sharp, tore through the crops with unnatural force. And among them, a small white rabbit, its eyes glowing like embers, darted with terrifying speed and precision, its teeth bared.

Wakamono drew his katana, the familiar weight of the blade steadying his mind. There was no time to think, no time to question. He rushed toward the fray, his blade flashing in the dim light, ready to defend his family from the madness that had descended on them.

九

A SUDDEN GUST OF wind swept through the trees, and with it came the first of the creatures—a twisted deer, its antlers gnarled and sharp as blades. It charged from the shadows with a guttural snarl, its eyes glowing, leaving a trail of corruption in its wake. Behind it, birds with tattered wings screeched through the air, their glowing eyes cutting through the darkness.

And then, from the shadows, came the kamikiri.

The creatures moved like the wind—small, hunched figures with long, bony arms ending in scythe-like claws that gleamed in the moonlight. Their faces were hidden beneath matted hair, but their mouths twisted into grotesque grins as they slashed at the air, hungry for flesh. Their movements were erratic, their bodies light and fast, almost blending with the shadows as they circled the farm.

Wakamono felt his muscles tense. He had heard stories of the kamikiri—spirits that once trimmed hair with mischievous intent. But these were different. Corrupted by the malevolent force in the forest, they had become savage, their claws no longer tools for pranks but weapons of destruction.

The first one lunged at him, its claw slicing through the air with a high-pitched whistle. Wakamono twisted to the side, the grotesque appendage missing him by inches as he brought his katana up in a swift arc. The creature shrieked as the blade connected with its side, sending it tumbling to the ground. But it didn't stay down for long.

Wakamono's breath came in quick bursts as he fought back the kamikiri, slashing at the creatures as they darted in and out of the shadows. His movements were precise, but the pain from his burns flared with each strike, his body reminding him that he was not fully healed.

A second kamikiri lunged at him from the side, its claw aimed for his throat. Wakamono barely had time to deflect the blow, the creature's sharp edge grazing his arm as he turned and drove his katana into its chest. It let out a horrible screech as it dropped lifelessly to the ground, but there were more coming.

His chest heaved with exertion, his hand trembling slightly as he prepared for the next attack. Every movement was a battle against the exhaustion pulling at his limbs. But he couldn't stop. Not now. Not with so much at stake.

後見

Red Mist moved through the chaos like a shadow—silent, swift, and deadly. Her katana gleamed in the dim light of the farm's lanterns, each strike a blur of motion that cut through the corrupted creatures with surgical precision.

A twisted deer charged at her, its jagged antlers aimed for her chest. Red Mist didn't flinch. With a swift sidestep, she avoided the beast's charge and brought her katana down in a clean, fluid arc. The blade sliced through the creature's neck effortlessly, sending its corrupted form collapsing to the ground with a thud. She barely spared it a glance before turning her attention to the next threat.

The kamikiri circled her, their claws gleaming as they slashed at the air, looking for an opening. But Red Mist gave them none.

Her movements were calculated, her focus absolute. Every step she took was measured, her katana always poised to strike. When one kamikiri lunged at her from the left, she blocked its claw with ease, twisting her wrist to deflect the blow and drive the creature back. Another kamikiri leaped from the shadows behind her, but before its claws could reach her, she spun around, her blade cutting through the air, and the beast, with deadly precision. The creature thudded to the cultivated soil, its screech swallowed by the wind.

There was no hesitation in her strikes, no wasted movement. Red Mist had spent years honing her skills, mastering the art of combat until every motion felt natural, effortless. She could feel the weight of the corruption pressing down on them, the malevolent force thickening the air, but she kept her mind sharp, her emotions in check. There was no room for doubt here.

A twisted deer charged at her, its glowing eyes filled with rage. Red Mist's gaze locked on it, her face unreadable as she prepared to meet its attack. At the last second, she stepped to the side, her katana flashing in the dim light as she sliced through the creature's legs. It collapsed, thrashing in the dirt, but before it could recover, Red Mist ended its suffering with a swift, clean strike to the neck.

Around her, the battle raged on. Wakamono fought valiantly despite his exhaustion, and she could hear the sounds of Hokori and Baka struggling against the onslaught. But Red Mist was the anchor of the fight, her composure and precision holding the line against the chaos.

A kamikiri darted toward her from the shadows, its claws aimed for her throat. Red Mist moved with lightning speed, her katana meeting the creature's attack with a sharp metallic clang. She twisted her wrist, deflecting the blow before driving the tip of her blade into the kamikiri's chest.

But despite their victories, Red Mist could feel the battle taking its toll. The corruption in the air was oppressive, thickening with every passing moment. Even as they cut down the creatures, more seemed to emerge from the darkness, their glowing eyes reflecting the malevolent force driving them forward.

Red Mist's eyes narrowed, her grip tightening on her katana. She knew they couldn't let this continue. The battle was far from over, and the weight of the malevolent force was pressing down on them all.

後見

Hokori stood at the edge of the battle, gripping the handle of a rusted garden rake, his knuckles white with tension. He wasn't a warrior—never had been, and never wanted to be. But as the corrupted creatures descended on the farm, he knew he couldn't stand by and watch them tear apart everything he had worked so hard to build.

The first creature that charged at him was a bird, its wings ragged and tattered, its glowing red eyes fixed on him with malevolent intent. Hokori swung the rake wildly, the metal teeth barely grazing the bird as it swooped past him. He cursed under his breath, his heart pounding in his chest. He didn't have the training or the reflexes of a Kōken. But he had strength—years of working the farm had made sure of that.

The bird came back around, diving toward him again, and this time, Hokori was ready. He swung the rake with all his might, the metal teeth catching the bird mid-flight. There was a sickening crunch as its body crumpled to the ground, twitching in the dirt. Hokori didn't have time to celebrate the small victory. Another creature, a twisted deer, barreled toward him, its jagged antlers gleaming in the moonlight.

Hokori braced himself, gripping the rake like a spear as the deer closed in. His muscles screamed in protest as he thrust the rake forward, aiming for the creature's chest. The jagged antlers scraped against his arm as the deer stumbled back, a glancing blow that sent pain shooting up his side. Blood dripped from the shallow wound, but Hokori gritted his teeth and forced himself to keep fighting.

He swung the rake again, this time connecting with the deer's neck. The creature let out a guttural snarl before collapsing to the ground, twitching as it took its last breath. Hokori panted heavily, his chest rising and falling with exertion. His movements were clumsy compared to Wakamono and Red Mist, but his raw strength was enough to keep him in the fight.

The battle raged around him, the sounds of screeching birds and the clash of blades filling the air. Hokori swung wildly at the creatures that came too close, his muscles burning with effort. His body wasn't built for this—his movements were reflexive and unrefined, and every swing of the rake felt like a gamble. But he refused to give up.

Another bird dove at him, its claws outstretched, but this time, Hokori was ready. He swung his crude weapon, the sharp metal catching the bird in midair and sending it tumbling to the ground. He didn't pause to admire his handiwork. He kept moving, kept fighting, even as the scratches on his arms and legs stung with every movement.

In the chaos, Hokori's eyes locked with Waka-mono's. For a brief moment, everything else seemed to fade—the noise, the blood, the violence. There was no resentment in Hokori's gaze, no anger. Just determination. He was fighting for the same cause as his brother. Despite their differences, despite the tension that had always simmered between them, they both knew what was at stake. Their home. Their family.

Hokori's grip tightened on the rake as he nodded once, a silent acknowledgment that they were in this together. Then he turned back to the battle, swinging the rake with renewed vigor as another wave of creatures surged toward him.

後見

Baka had always been the gentle one. His strength, though formidable from years of hard labor on the farm, had never been something he wielded with aggression. But tonight, the sight of his home under siege, the twisted creatures clawing at the life he had known, stirred something deep inside him. Something primal. Something fierce.

He watched as the corrupted animals tore through the farm—birds with glowing eyes, deer with jagged antlers, and those strange, clawed creatures that moved like shadows. They were attacking everything he loved. They were attacking his family.

A low growl built in Baka's throat, his large hands balling into fists. The usual simple, placid expression on his face twisted with anger. Without thinking, he grabbed a heavy stone from the ground and hurled it at one of the birds swooping low over the farmhouse. The stone struck with a sickening thud, knocking the creature from the sky in a flurry of tattered wings and feathers.

His breath came in ragged bursts as the rage surged through him, turning the normally kind-hearted man into a force of raw emotion. His muscles tightened, fueled by the adrenaline coursing through his veins. He had no training, no knowledge of how to fight like

Wakamono or Red Mist, but none of that mattered now. His only thought was to protect his family. Protect his home.

With a guttural roar, Baka grabbed a rusted shovel from the ground and swung it with all his might at one of the twisted deer charging toward the barn. The metal blade connected with the creature's side, the force of the blow sending it sprawling into the dirt. The deer struggled to rise, its corrupted body twitching, but Baka didn't give it the chance. He brought the shovel down again, dealing a killing blow.

He was breathing hard now, his chest heaving with the effort, but the fury driving him forward was relentless. His usually soft brown eyes were alight with something wild and fierce, something that had been unseen in him before. He didn't care about technique or precision—he just wanted to destroy.

A bird dove toward him, its claws outstretched, but Baka swung his arm with surprising speed, catching the creature mid-flight with the back of his hand. It screeched as it hit the ground, and Baka stomped down with all the force he could muster, silencing it.

More of the twisted creatures closed in, but Baka, in his frenzy, was ready. He grabbed whatever he could—tools, stones, even broken pieces of debris—and hurled them with shocking accuracy at the advancing enemies. His blows were wild, uncontrolled, but each one hit with a force that could shatter bones. A nearby deer stumbled under his assault, one of its jagged antlers broken clean off from the impact of a heavy hand.

In the midst of the chaos, Baka let out a bellowing roar, his fury driving him forward. His love for his family fueled every swing of his arm, every step he took. He was clumsy and untrained, but the sheer power behind his attacks made him a force of nature. The creatures fell under his onslaught, their corrupted bodies unable to withstand the strength of his rage.

He wasn't thinking—he couldn't think. His mind was lost in the storm of emotion, the need to protect, the need to destroy the evil that had invaded his home. Every time he swung, every time he struck down another twisted creature, he thought of his brothers, of Bi, of the life they had built together. He couldn't let these creatures take that away.

With one brutal swing of the shovel, Baka sent a deer crashing into the side of the barn, its body crumpling in a heap. He stood there, panting, his chest rising and falling with the effort, his hands shaking from the sheer power of his own fury.

But even as the last of the creatures fell around him, Baka's eyes scanned the farm, searching for the next threat, his rage still burning beneath the surface. He wasn't done. Not until his family was safe.

後見

The farmstead was eerily still, the chaotic clamor of battle replaced by a heavy, oppressive silence. The bodies of the corrupted animals lay scattered across the fields, their twisted forms lifeless, their jagged limbs bent at unnatural angles. Dark blood seeped into the soil, a reminder of the ferocity that had just unfolded.

Wakamono stood in the center of the carnage, his breath coming in ragged gasps. Blood trickled from a gash on his arm, mingling with the sweat that dripped from his exhausted body. His katana, still gripped tightly in his hand, was slick with the dark ichor of the creatures they had slain. His muscles ached, and the familiar sting of exhaustion settled deep in his bones, but they had survived. They had won.

Nearby, Red Mist stood motionless, her katana at her side, the tip of the blade resting lightly on the ground. Her expression was as stoic as ever, but her sharp eyes betrayed a flicker of weariness. Her dark hair, disheveled from the fight, clung to her face in strands, but she showed no sign of slowing down. Her strikes had been precise, her movements measured, but even she couldn't deny the weight of the battle that had just taken place.

Across the field, Hokori knelt in the dirt, breathing heavily, clutching his bruised side. His hands trembled as he wiped away the blood from a scratch on his face, his garden rake lying discarded beside him. He was battered and bruised, but still alive. Despite the pain, despite the fear, he had fought alongside his brothers.

Baka stood nearby, his massive frame heaving as he struggled to catch his breath. His face was flushed with the effort of battle, his usually gentle eyes wide with lingering rage. His hands were still shaking from the power of his attacks, the raw emotion that had driven him forward now leaving him feeling empty, his fury spent. The farm tools he had wielded so viciously lay scattered at his feet, covered in dirt and blood.

The last of the kamikiri spirits retreated into the darkness, their forms dissolving into the night. Their eerie, clawed silhouettes vanished as quickly as they had appeared, leaving only a faint whisper of malevolent energy behind. But even as they faded from view, the corruption in the air remained—heavy, oppressive, clinging to the very earth beneath their feet.

The silence that followed the battle was thick, the weight of the corruption still pressing down on the farm. Wakamono's gaze swept across the fields, taking in the destruction—the torn earth, the broken bodies of the creatures they had fought. It wasn't over. This battle, this victory, was only a small part of a much larger war. He could feel it in his bones.

Red Mist's eyes met his, her expression unreadable, but there was an unspoken understanding between them. They had fought valiantly, and they had won, but the danger was far from gone. The malevolent force that had twisted these creatures was still out there, lurking in the shadows, waiting to strike again.

Wakamono looked to his brothers. Hokori, bruised and battered but alive. Baka, still panting from the exertion but standing tall. They had all fought for their home, for their family, and for now, they had succeeded. But this was just the beginning. Whatever malevolence had brought this corruption to their doorstep was still out there, and they would have to face it.

The wind rustled through the fields, carrying with it the faintest echo of the battle they had just fought. It was a reminder of the darkness still looming over them, a warning of the greater threat that awaited.

Wakamono sheathed his katana, the weight of it a familiar comfort against his side. He exchanged a glance with Red Mist, the faintest nod passing between them. The battle had been won, but the war was far from over.

10+

THE NIGHT WAS STILL, the chaos of battle fading into an eerie silence that settled over the farm. The twisted bodies of corrupted animals lay strewn across the fields, their jagged forms motionless under the pale moonlight. The air was thick with the smell of blood and damp earth, and the quiet felt fragile, like the calm after a storm.

From the shadows, the villagers slowly emerged. At first, they came in ones and twos, their faces pale and drawn, eyes wide with disbelief at the destruction laid before them. Some stepped closer to the farm's edge, keeping their distance from the lifeless bodies. Others huddled in doorways, whispering to one another as they took in the sight of Wakamono and Red Mist standing bloodied but victorious.

An old man, bent with age but still gripping a farming hoe with trembling hands, shuffled closer. His gaze shifted from the fallen creatures to Wakamono and Red Mist. "The Kōken saved us," he muttered under his breath, his voice barely above a whisper.

There was gratitude in his eyes, but also something darker—something uncertain.

A murmur rippled through the gathered villagers, low and uneasy.

"Why did they come here?" a woman's voice broke through the quiet, sharp with fear. She stood clutching her child to her chest, her eyes darting between the bodies and the warriors who had fought them. "We've never seen anything like this before."

"They bring trouble with them," another voice answered from deeper in the crowd. A middle-aged man stepped forward, his brow furrowed in suspicion. "These Kōken—they draw the darkness to them. Always have."

The words hung in the air, the tension growing as more villagers began to voice their concerns. Fear was taking hold, turning into something more dangerous—anger. Wakamono's muscles tensed as he listened to the murmurs rise. His heart still pounded from the battle, the adrenaline coursing through him, but now his mind was focused on something else: the creeping realization that the people he had come to protect were beginning to question his very presence.

"They saved us," the old man repeated, his voice shaking slightly. But his words did little to calm the rising tide of fear.

"They bring danger," a woman bit out, her voice laced with bitterness. "Wherever the Kōken go, evil follows."

Wakamono's chest tightened. He had heard this before, from others who didn't understand the burden the Kōken carried—the weight of protecting those who couldn't protect themselves. He glanced at Red Mist, who stood quietly beside him, her expression unreadable. But he could feel the villagers' eyes on him, the weight of their suspicions pressing down like a physical force.

Suddenly beside them, Hokori's voice rang out, low but firm. "They're not wrong, Waka."

Wakamono's breath hitched, and he turned to face his brother. Hokori's face was set in a hard line, his arms crossed tightly over his chest. His words were deliberate, each one dripping with accusation.

"They came for you," Hokori said, stepping forward slowly, toward the forming crowd, his gaze fixed on Wakamono. "These creatures, this corruption—it's not a coincidence. You brought this down on us."

Wakamono felt a flare of anger, but also something deeper—guilt, perhaps, though he fought to push it aside. "I came to protect you," he replied, his voice steady, though his chest felt heavy. "That's what we do. That's what the Kōken do."

Hokori let out a bitter laugh, shaking his head. "Protect us? Look around, Waka." He gestured to the ruined fields, the fallen creatures. "This farm, our home—it's all in ruins. You may think you're protecting us, but all I see is more danger, more destruction. Before you arrived, all we had to deal with were some sick plants."

Wakamono's heart raced, a knot forming in his stomach as the weight of Hokori's words settled over him. He opened his mouth to respond, but the anger, the frustration—it stuck in his throat.

"You think I wanted this?" Wakamono said, his voice low but fierce. "You think I don't see what's happened here? But if we weren't here, it would have been worse. The Kōken fight because we have to. We can't let these things destroy everything."

Hokori's eyes flashed with anger. "And yet, they came for you. Not us. You."

The villagers had grown quiet again, watching the exchange between the brothers with bated breath. The tension between them felt palpable, the air thick with years of unspoken resentment. Wakamono could see it in his brother's face—the pain, the frustration, the fear that had been festering since their father's death.

And then, in a voice barely above a whisper, the elderly woman stepped forward. "Thank you, Gou," she said softly, her eyes distant, lost in memory. "We're all safer having an ex-soldier like you nearby. I'll bring some anpan over for you wife and children. Such a sweet family," she muttered, as a young woman gently pulled her away.

Wakamono froze at the mention of their father, the words cutting deeper than any blade. Hokori's face twisted into something pained, his lips parting as if to speak. But he stopped himself, the words dying on his tongue. For a moment, Wakamono saw the raw emotion flicker in his brother's eyes—the hurt, the anger, the unspoken grief that had been simmering just beneath the surface.

Hokori clenched his fists, his knuckles white. He was on the verge of saying something more, something that would tear open the wounds they had both been avoiding. But then, Baka stumbled out from the farmhouse, his face pale and drawn.

The cold, furious expression he wore during the attack was replaced with one of fear, his eyes wide and unfocused as he looked around at the devastation. His hands shook as he wiped them on his tunic, his breath coming in shallow gasps.

"Waka..." Baka's voice trembled. "Is it over? Are... are they gone?"

The sight of Baka's fear—the sheer vulnerability in his voice—was enough to shatter the tension between the brothers. Wakamono's anger melted away, replaced by a fierce protectiveness. He moved toward Baka, placing a steadying hand on his shoulder, offering what little comfort he could.

Hokori, too, seemed to deflate, his shoulders slumping as he watched his younger brother struggle to comprehend the night's events. The fire of their argument extinguished, leaving behind only the unspoken understanding that they couldn't afford to fight among themselves. Not now.

Wakamono caught Hokori's eye, and for a moment, neither of them spoke. No apologies were exchanged, no promises made. But there was a quiet truce between them, a mutual agreement to set aside their differences—at least, for the time being.

As the villagers slowly dispersed, the weight of the night's events settled over the farm like a heavy cloak. The battle was over, but the real fight had only just begun.

+一

THE FOREST AROUND KAIDA had changed. What was once vibrant with the sounds of life now lay shrouded in a heavy, unnatural silence. The trees, tall and ancient, no longer stood proudly but seemed to twist and groan under an invisible weight. Their bark was split, darkened with rot, and in places, tendrils of blackened vines coiled around the trunks like serpents, choking the very life from them.

Kaida walked slowly, each step deliberate. The ground beneath him was soft and unstable, as though it might crumble away at any moment. Fallen leaves, once golden with the autumn chill, now crunched underfoot with a brittle, diseased texture. The smell of decay filled the air—a sharp contrast to the crisp scent that had once carried through the gorge. But it was not the sight or the stench that troubled Kaida; it was the feeling.

The air thrummed with malevolence. It was a sensation that most would overlook, a subtle shifting in the atmosphere that hinted at the wrongness festering

97

within the land. But Kaida, with his deep connection to the spiritual world, felt it acutely. Every breath he took was heavy with corruption. The earth beneath his feet groaned with each step as though protesting the weight of its burden.

He paused, his eyes narrowing as he scanned the forest ahead. The trees, gnarled and twisted, leaned toward him in unnatural arcs. The branches reached out like skeletal fingers, their leaves curled and brown, as if the vitality had been siphoned from them long ago. The wind barely stirred, as though it, too, was trapped in the weight of the forest's slow death.

There was no fear in Kaida's heart. His spirit, honed through years of meditation and solitude, remained steady, unshaken by the decay that surrounded him. He was not unfamiliar with the signs of corruption, though he had not felt it this strong in many years. His pace slowed as he approached a particularly large tree, its roots swollen and cracked, spilling into the dirt like a festering wound.

Kaida crouched beside the tree, placing a hand gently on the bark. The rough texture of the wood crumbled beneath his fingers, and yet beneath the decay, he could feel the faint pulse of life struggling to survive. The tree's spirit was wounded, its energy sapped by the dark forces that had invaded the forest.

"Hmm..." Kaida muttered, his voice low and rough, as if speaking to the earth itself. "The leaves whisper of sickness, but the roots know more..."

He closed his eyes, allowing the faint energy of the tree to flow into him. His mind's eye reached deeper into the earth, searching for the source of the corruption. The darkness was pervasive, tendrils of malice spreading like poison through the soil, but something in the distance tugged at his senses—something far greater than this single tree.

"Distant, but not far enough... waiting." His voice trailed off as he stood, brushing the decayed wood from his hand. His eyes scanned the treetops, sharp despite his age, and he could feel the sky itself tremble under the weight of the corruption. Whatever was festering here, it was not simply an affliction of nature—it was something darker, something far older than the forest itself.

He turned to continue his journey, but paused as a flicker of movement caught his eye. Just ahead, stepping through the underbrush, was a deer. But it was no ordinary creature. Its once graceful form was twisted and mangled, its fur matted with filth and dark streaks running along its sides like black veins. Its eyes, once bright with life, were clouded with a red haze, and its antlers were jagged, grown misshapen under the influence of the corruption.

Kaida remained still, watching the creature with calm focus. He held no fear, only a deep sadness for the suffering of the animal. The deer, too, was a victim of the darkness that had crept into the forest, and its presence here was a testament to how far the corruption had spread.

Without a word, Kaida took a step forward, his hand already reaching for the creature, knowing what he must do.

Kaida stepped forward with calm deliberation, his every movement measured and purposeful. The corrupted buck shifted its head toward him, its red eyes glowing dimly beneath the shadow of its twisted antlers. A low, guttural noise escaped the creature's throat—a sound more akin to the creaking of ancient wood than an animal's cry. It pawed the ground, the motion unnatural and jerking, as if it no longer fully understood how to move.

Kaida's eyes softened with pity. The creature was suffering, a victim ensnared by forces it could not comprehend, caught in the grip of something far beyond its nature. He stepped closer, now only a few feet away, the deer's head twitching erratically as if trying to focus through the haze clouding its mind. It staggered, but did not charge. The malevolence that filled the creature held it in thrall, even as its body buckled under the weight of the corruption.

Kaida extended his hand, the lines of his palm steady. His fingers hovered over the deer's head, his touch gentle but sure as his palm made contact with the matted fur. The creature stilled under his hand, its body trembling as if recognizing the presence of something greater than itself, something that brought with it a fleeting feeling of peace.

The old man closed his eyes, drawing in a slow breath as the forest seemed to still around him. He could feel the corruption pulsating through the deer's veins, like thick tar slowly suffocating the spirit that once animated this animal. It was a darkness he had felt before, though never this concentrated. His brow furrowed, and he whispered softly to the creature, his words carrying the weight of a long-forgotten tranquility.

"Beneath twisted roots,
Silent strength heals what is lost,
Rest now, weary soul."

As the final word left his mouth, a ripple of energy surged through the deer. The red glow in its eyes flickered, dimmed, and then vanished entirely. The tension in its muscles eased, and for a moment, Kaida could feel the creature's spirit—untethered from the corruption—begin to rise. It was as if the very essence of the deer was being released from its bonds.

But with that release came the inevitable. The deer, once held together by the dark energy coursing through its veins, collapsed at Kaida's feet. The body, now free of the corruption, could no longer sustain itself. It had been too long under the grip of darkness. Kaida knelt beside it, his hand still resting on the creature's head as its breathing slowed, then stopped.

He bowed his head slightly, his expression serene yet somber. The corruption had taken so much from this forest, and this deer was only one of many. It had been freed from the grip of malevolence, but the cost was its life—a price Kaida knew was necessary to halt the spread, at least for now.

For a long moment, Kaida remained still, letting the stillness settle around him. The forest, though corrupted, seemed to respond to his presence, a quiet acknowledgment of the balance he had restored in this small corner of the woods.

Rising to his feet, Kaida spared one last glance at the fallen deer before continuing on his path. There was no time for mourning, not now. The source of this corruption was still out there, twisting and spreading through the roots of the forest, deeper than even he could yet fathom. He walked on, his pace steady and calm, knowing the battle ahead was not one of brute force, but of spirit and endurance.

As he made his way deeper into the forest, the trees once again closed in around him, their shadows stretching long and dark under the pale autumn sky. Kaida knew he had only scratched the surface of what lay ahead. And though his heart was heavy with the knowledge of the suffering yet to be uncovered, his resolve did not waver.

His thoughts shifted, and as he stepped over the corrupted roots and gnarled branches, a faint sound caught his attention—something distant, carried on the wind. He paused, tilting his head slightly. It was faint, barely noticeable at first, but there, unmistakable. The clashing of hardened steel. A distant cry, muffled by the thick trees but sharp enough to reach his ears.

A battle was raging.

Kaida's expression remained calm, though his eyes narrowed slightly. He had expected this. The corruption of the forest would not go unchallenged, not if others like him had sensed the darkness creeping across the land. The sounds were far off, but they confirmed what Kaida had already suspected: the source of this corruption was drawing those who would fight against it.

Adjusting his cloak, he began to walk again, his steps slow but deliberate as he made his way toward the sound of battle. He would meet it in time, not as a warrior seeking glory, but as a seer following the threads of fate that had woven themselves into this forest.

+二

WAKAMONO STOOD AT THE edge of the farm, his eyes scanning the fields that had once been his childhood home. Now, they were scarred by the night's battle—broken bodies of corrupted animals and twisted spirits scattered across the ground. The quiet of the early morning felt heavy, as if the land itself hadn't recovered from the chaos that had swept over it just hours before.

He glanced toward Red Mist, who was silently fastening the straps of her light armor. She moved with the same calm precision as always, unaffected by the destruction around them. Wakamono, on the other hand, couldn't shake the frustration that gnawed at him.

"Bi asked for our help, but I'm starting to wonder if I should've come at all," Wakamono muttered, his voice low. "Hokori doesn't want me here. He made that clear enough. And Baka…" He trailed off, clenching his fists at the memory. "Baka could've gotten himself killed, charging in like that. He's got no training, no sense, and yet he throws himself into the fight like it's nothing."

Red Mist didn't look up from her preparations, but he knew she was listening.

"I thought they needed me," Wakamono continued, his frustration building. "But Hokori—he acts like I'm more of a problem than a solution. And Baka—he's my brother, but sometimes I feel like I'm just here to clean up his mess."

Red Mist paused, her fingers tightening the last strap of her armor. "Family has a way of being complicated," she said, her tone as even as ever.

Wakamono scoffed. "That's putting it lightly."

Red Mist finally turned to him, her gaze steady. "Though, I wouldn't know."

The quiet weight of her words made Wakamono pause. He looked at her, really looked at her, and saw the reality she spoke of—a life without family's bonds or burdens. Her world had been one of survival and isolation, shaped by hardship and solitude.

He opened his mouth to speak, but Red Mist continued, her voice calm but firm. "You have a family to fight for. They're flawed. They make mistakes, but don't we all? Even so, they're yours." She adjusted the katana at her side, her gaze never leaving his. "I don't know what that's like. But I do know that, for all their faults, they're part of why you're still fighting."

Wakamono shifted, the weight of her words settling in. He had come to the farm to protect his family, to fight for them, but his brother's resentment and his own frustration had clouded his purpose. He let out a breath, letting the anger settle, feeling a measure of clarity.

"I guess I've been so focused on the fights in front of me that I forgot about what I'm really fighting for," Wakamono admitted, his voice softer now.

Red Mist gave a slight nod. "The battlefield can make everything else seem distant. But don't forget that this"—she gestured to the land, the farm, the remnants of the battle—"is why you're here. It's why we're here. For your family. For those who can't fight for themselves."

Wakamono sighed, feeling the tension in his chest ease just a little. "I just wish it didn't feel like I'm fighting two battles—one against this evil, and one against my own family."

"No one said it would be easy," she replied, an almost imperceptible twitch at the corner of her mouth. "In fact, we know the opposite to be true."

Wakamono let out a small, dry chuckle. "I suppose."

Red Mist finished tightening the last buckle on her armor and stood up. "We leave at dawn. Get as much rest as you can, but be ready."

Wakamono nodded, watching as she turned to pack the rest of her gear. He took one last look at the farm, the home that had become both a battleground and a reminder of the people he was fighting for.

後見

As the first light crept over the horizon, Wakamono adjusted the last strap on his armor, the quiet air around him heavy with anticipation. Just as he was about to hoist his pack onto his shoulder, he noticed Hokori approaching. His older brother moved slowly, nursing a bruise on his shoulder, his face etched with exhaustion from the night's battle.

Hokori's gaze lingered on Wakamono, but his eyes held a conflicted mix of emotions—resentment and guilt shadowing his expression. He stood there in silence, his mouth pressed into a thin line, as if debating whether to speak. The strain between them hung uncomfortably in the air, like a wound neither was ready to address.

Wakamono felt the weight of Hokori's unspoken words, the way his brother looked at him as though he wanted to say something, to resolve whatever lay between them. But there was no time now, and Wakamono knew it. Duty came first.

"Take care of things here," he said simply, keeping his voice steady, his words meant as much for himself as for Hokori. A subtle reminder that they both had roles to play.

Hokori gave a curt nod, his gaze hardening as he looked away. "You don't have to remind me, little brother. I've been taking care of the farm while you've been... away. You do what you have to do, Kōken." His tone was neutral, but there was an edge to it, a lingering bitterness that made Wakamono's chest tighten. Hokori turned away, leaving the words unsaid, and Wakamono was left with the ache of knowing his brother's wounds went deeper than the bruises on his body.

Just then, Baka appeared, bounding up to Wakamono with a beaming smile despite the dried blood and dirt still smeared across his cheeks. He held out a cloth bundle, his eyes alight with the same cheerful energy he always carried, unbroken even by the horrors of the night before.

"I brought you some of the good rice balls," Baka said proudly, handing the bundle to Wakamono as though it were a prize. "You'll need them for your journey. And don't worry about things here—I'll keep an eye on Hokori." He gave a wink, as if the previous night's chaos was nothing more than a small bump in the road.

A small, reluctant smile tugged at Wakamono's lips as he took the bundle from Baka. His brother's simple optimism was like a balm, reminding him of the days before Kōken training, before battles with akuma and the scars left by duty. Baka's presence was a reminder of what he was fighting for, the innocence and re-silience of his family—something pure that he wished to protect.

"Thanks, Baka," he said, his tone softer. "I'll be back."

Baka grinned, clapping Wakamono on the shoulder with enough force to make him stagger. "Just don't forget the way home. You were gone too long, last time."

Wakamono chuckled, his heart feeling a little lighter. He adjusted his pack, casting one last look at his family—the brother he wished to mend things with, and the one who seemed blissfully untouched by the darkness surrounding them.

As he turned to join Red Mist at the edge of the farm, he felt a renewed determination settle within him. No matter the battles ahead, he would protect them. For Baka's bright spirit. For Hokori's silent struggle. For all of them.

後見

The sun barely filtered through the dense canopy as Wakamono and Red Mist entered the forest, their steps swallowed by the damp earth and rotting foliage. The air grew colder and thick with the stench of de-cay, a sour undercurrent that made Wakamono's skin prickle with unease. Every step felt as though it took them deeper into a living nightmare.

Red Mist broke the silence, her tone steady but her gaze sharp as she scanned the shadows. "Remember, we're not just here for your family. The entire village—and more beyond it—is at risk. This corruption... it's growing. We need to find its source before it spreads any further."

Wakamono nodded, gripping his katana as his gaze swept the twisted trees around them. "I saw what it did to the animals. If it reaches the main farmlands, the damage will be immeasurable."

Red Mist's voice softened but held a wary edge. "And there's something else you should know. Last night, I wasn't alone in my meditations." She paused, letting her words settle before continuing. "Yama-uba appeared to me."

Wakamono's eyes widened, his body tensed. Yama-uba—the witch whose cryptic guidance, or misguidance, he knew all too well. Her warnings had haunted him since she first appeared in his path, always with that twisted smile and promises of insight shrouded in riddles.

"What did she say this time?" he asked, trying to mask the unease in his voice.

"She warned of something more sinister than we've faced before," Red Mist replied, her tone more somber than he was used to hearing. "She spoke of you in particular, Wakamono. Suggested that you're in danger—that we both are. She was... pleased by the thought, if I had to guess."

Wakamono's brow furrowed, anger stirring within him. "She's never helpful, only hinting at what she wants me to fear. She's trying to make us doubt ourselves, to weaken us."

"True," Red Mist acknowledged, "but her warnings are rarely empty. She doesn't have to lie to achieve her ends. She thrives on twisting the truth just enough to leave us questioning."

Wakamono's jaw tightened. "So, what do we do?"

Red Mist turned her gaze back to the trees, her expression unreadable. "We stay vigilant. She hinted that the corruption we're seeing is only the beginning of something more—something that will test both of us."

Wakamono nodded, steeling himself. "Then we move forward, and we do our duty."

They pressed deeper into the forest, and the air grew thicker, more oppressive. Shadows hung over them like a living shroud, and the very trees around them seemed to sag under the weight of some unseen illness. Branches hung low, their bark blackened and peeling away in strips. Leaves dangled like shriveled claws, brittle and gray, reaching to tear at any passerby.

At their feet, the underbrush was littered with carcasses—small animals, their bodies twisted and misshapen, lying scattered across the forest floor as if discarded. Wakamono spotted a mangled fox, its fur matted and limbs bent at unnatural angles, its eyes wide and unseeing. A few steps later, he stumbled over a deer, its antlers jagged and misshapen, as if twisted by some unseen force.

Red Mist's eyes scanned their surroundings, her face impassive but her grip on her katana steady. "This is unnatural. It's something malignant, something that's thriving on the decay."

Wakamono's gaze hardened as he took in the scene. "Whatever it is, it needs to be stopped before it consumes everything."

With a nod, Red Mist moved forward, her form steady as she led the way through the darkening forest. And as they stepped further into the shadows, the twisted remnants of the once-living seemed to close in around them, a grim reminder of the price of hesitation.

The path ahead was dark, but their resolve was stronger still.

13
十三

THE AIR GREW COLDER, a strange chill settling around them as they ventured deeper into the forest. Mist clung to the ground, weaving between the roots and creeping around the bases of trees twisted into unnatural shapes, their branches reaching like skeletal fingers clawing at the pale morning light. The familiar sounds of the forest—birdsong, rustling leaves, the hum of life—had disappeared, replaced by an oppressive silence broken only by faint, unsettling scuttling noises echoing off the damp trees.

Wakamono's steps slowed as he took in the warped landscape around him. The trees' bark, usually rough and alive with moss, was now blackened and peeling, giving way to webs that stretched across their trunks. But these webs were not like those spun by ordinary spiders; they were thick, coarse, and dark, almost as if the forest itself had been woven into some sinister trap. Dew clung to the strands, catching the faint light and casting an unnatural, ghostly glow across the forest.

He tightened his grip on his katana, his senses sharpened. Every shadow seemed to shift, every flicker of movement in the mist carrying the potential for danger. He glanced sideways at Red Mist, her figure a calm anchor amid the corruption around them. She held her katana loosely, her posture relaxed but purposeful, her eyes sharp and alert, taking in every detail. Wakamono found himself steadying at her presence. For all his training, he recognized he was still learning the balance of alertness and calm. Watching her unwavering composure, he felt a growing respect, a realization of the strength that years of practice had brought her.

"Do you sense it?" he murmured, his voice barely a whisper, as though afraid to disturb the silence.

Red Mist nodded, her eyes scanning the path ahead. "Stay close. There's something lurking here… something that doesn't belong."

The faint scuttling grew louder, a chittering noise just on the edge of hearing, as though whatever awaited them was aware of their approach. The mist thickened, and Wakamono could feel a weight constricting his body, a creeping unease that seemed to seep from the ground itself.

They pressed onward, the forest growing darker with each step, until finally, Wakamono stopped, his instincts telling him they had entered a place of even deeper danger. Red Mist's eyes met his briefly, a look of acknowledgment passing between them. Whatever was out there was close, and Wakamono felt a flicker of gratitude for her presence, knowing her steadiness would be crucial as they moved forward into the unknown.

The mist seemed to thicken around them, obscuring the distant trees as Wakamono carefully scanned his surroundings. His senses were on edge, every muscle poised for action, when suddenly, a shadow dropped from above.

With a sickening thud, something massive collided with him, knocking him back onto the damp forest floor. As he hit the ground, Wakamono struggled to breathe, his chest heaving against the weight that held him down. As he was rapidly spun, thick, sticky threads wrapped around him, pinning his arms to his sides and immobilizing his legs. He writhed, but the webbing only clung tighter, each movement binding him more securely.

A grotesque shape loomed overhead—the tsuchigumo. The creature's body was huge, almost the size of a full-grown bear, with bristly legs that clawed into the ground on either side of him. Its eyes, disturbingly bulbous and glassy, shimmered with a sickly yellow hue, catching the faint light filtering through the mist. The eyes, unnervingly human-like, darted over him, a glint of malevolent intelligence flashing across them. Its mandibles, sharp and jagged, dripped with venom that hissed as it fell, sizzling against the underbrush.

The tsuchigumo's legs shifted, bristling hairs vibrating as it prepared to strike. Each movement sent a tremor through the ground beneath him, as though the very forest was quivering in anticipation. The creature's droning hum, emitted from deep within its body, grew louder, reverberating through the air and filling Wakamono's ears with an unbearable tension.

Pinned and helpless, panic flared within him, his breath quickening as he fought against the cloying, constrictive threads. But then, Red Mist's words echoed in his mind—a reminder to stay calm, to keep control. He closed his eyes, inhaling deeply, his fingers flexing instinctively as he forced himself to steady his breathing and block out the fear that clawed at his chest. He wouldn't give the beast the satisfaction of seeing him break. His pulse slowed, his focus sharpening as he searched for a way out.

The tsuchigumo loomed closer, mandibles clicking, venom dripping in anticipation. It paused, almost relishing the sight of him trapped, and then lowered its head further, preparing to strike.

Wakamono drew a slow, controlled breath, feeling the damp chill of the forest floor beneath him, pressing into his back. Instead of struggling, he forced his body to relax, his mind narrowing to a single, sharp focus. He shifted his hand toward the short blade wrapped against his hip, the motion barely perceptible. His fingers wrapped around the hilt, feeling the familiar weight, grounding him.

With a flick of his wrist, he angled the blade carefully, catching the webbing that held his wrist. The sticky threads fell away with a soft snap. His other hand freed, he moved methodically, cutting through each binding with minimal movement, keeping the tsuchigumo unaware. Its massive, arachnid form seemed distracted, each of its legs clicking and twitching, its eyes frantically scanning the area around it.

Wakamono took one last breath, feeling the weight of the forest's corruption pressing down on him, before slicing the last strand of webbing. As he rolled to his feet, blade at the ready, his eyes fell upon a shocking sight: Red Mist was surrounded by several monstrous tsuchigumo corpses, their bulbous forms twisted and lifeless on the forest floor, ichor pooling beneath them. She moved fluidly through the chaos, her katana gleaming as she turned to face another advancing beast.

It was then that he realized the danger he'd been in. The tsuchigumo that had trapped him was just one of several; Red Mist had been contending with them alone, her blade carving through each foe with unerring precision.

Just as he steadied himself, she plunged her katana through the head of the tsuchigumo that had ensnared him, its body crumpling as her blade severed its life force. Red Mist withdrew her sword with a practiced flick, turning her gaze briefly to Wakamono. There was no smile or nod, just a flicker of relief.

But the brief reprieve ended as another wave of the creatures emerged from the shadows, their chittering, scuttling movements echoing ominously through the corrupted forest. Wakamono replaced his short blade and drew his katana, his resolve steeling as he took his place beside Red Mist, prepared to meet the onslaught head-on. Together, they braced themselves for the next assault, the forest around them thick with malice and the promise of relentless battle.

The swarm of tsuchigumo closed in from all sides, their countless legs scratching across the forest floor in a maddening chorus. Wakamono steadied his breathing, his fingers gripping the hilt of his blade as he scanned the horde, positioning himself beside Red Mist.

Red Mist stood poised, her gaze calculating, as she nodded to Wakamono, giving a quick, silent cue. Without a word, they launched into the fray, her blade moving like a ribbon of steel, cutting through the air with controlled power. She sidestepped a lunging tsuchigumo, spinning to her right as her katana cleaved through the creature's thorax in a single stroke.

Wakamono matched her movements, though his strikes lacked her absolute precision. He was adjusting to the creatures' unpredictable lunges, each clawed leg stabbing forward like a spear. One creature charged him head-on, its eyes glinting as its fangs glistened with venom. He leaped sideways, his blade slicing down to sever one of its legs, but the tsuchigumo twisted mid-air, landing and snapping toward him with a haunting, guttural hiss.

Red Mist, already finishing off another creature, threw her gaze toward him and issued a brief, quiet signal with her free hand—*higher angle*. Wakamono adjusted, rolling his shoulders back and bringing his blade down in a clean arc, catching the creature at the base of its neck. The tsuchigumo crumpled, its legs twitching as it fell to the forest floor.

Wakamono's pulse raced, and he looked to Red Mist mist for approval only to find that she had already turned her attention to the next wave of attackers. She moved through the horde with elegance, her strikes so precise that each blow ended a creature in an instant. Her katana flashed in the dim, corrupted light, each slice like a line of silver in the shadows, while Wakamono worked to match her rhythm.

Another tsuchigumo lunged, aiming for his left side. He shifted quickly, bringing his blade up and across, the edge biting through the creature's hide. Though he was faster now, more disciplined, the sweat trickling down his back reminded him that he still had ground to cover. A moment's hesitation was all the time one tsuchigumo needed—it lunged, claws outstretched, and he felt a sting as one claw scraped his arm.

Gritting his teeth, he sidestepped the blow, pivoting on his back foot and driving his blade into the creature's exposed underbelly. He didn't wait to watch it fall. He spun toward another, catching sight of Red Mist sweeping past, a storm of silk threads and steel, leaving a trail of lifeless tsuchigumo in her wake. Her mastery was inspiring, each motion filled with lethal confidence, a balance he aspired to but hadn't yet fully achieved.

A brief nod of acknowledgment passed between them, and for a moment, he felt the intensity of the Kōken's true purpose: partnership, strength, and unwavering resolve. Together, they pressed forward, severing the final creatures' limbs, pushing back the relentless swarm until the forest was littered with the twisted bodies of the defeated tsuchigumo.

The forest fell silent, a stillness settling over the ground. Breathing heavily, Wakamono steadied himself, his gaze meeting Red Mist's. She inclined her head, an almost imperceptible nod of approval.

Red Mist and Wakamono moved quickly, weaving through the forest's twisted paths without pause. The faint traces of webs and tangled branches served as silent reminders of the ambush they had just survived.

Red Mist shot Wakamono a sidelong glance. "You handled yourself well enough back there," she said, her voice low and measured. "But don't let your guard down. Out here, one slip could mean everything."

Wakamono nodded, his jaw set with determination. The adrenaline from the battle still coursed through him, but he felt the weight of her words. "Understood."

They moved in silence after that, focused and watchful, each footfall bringing them deeper into the corrupted forest.

十四

THE FOREST LOOMED DARK and twisted as Wakamono and Red Mist continued their trek, moving
cautiously through the dense, corrupted wilderness.
A thick fog clung to the ground in stagnant pools,
creeping around the base of warped trees whose roots
jutted like broken bone fragments from the earth.
The air was thick and unwelcoming, carrying a sharp,
metallic tang that stung their senses. It felt unnatural,
and each breath tasted faintly of rot, as though the
very essence of the forest had been soured by some
unseen hand.

Wakamono felt a chill crawl up his spine. The trees
were more than just twisted; they seemed to bend
toward him as if they, too, were alive with malevolence. Gnarled branches intertwined overhead, casting a dense canopy that blotted out the light, leaving
the undergrowth bathed in perpetual dusk. Shadows
played tricks on his eyes, forming shapes that looked
almost human before melting back into the gloom.

Red Mist moved silently beside him, her posture taut but unafraid, her hand never far from her katana's hilt. She glanced briefly at Wakamono, giving a barely perceptible nod that spoke of her readiness. He returned the nod, steeling himself. In his hands, he gripped his blade a little tighter, eyes scanning the path ahead for any sign of movement.

Then, they saw her.

At the edge of the grove, partly hidden by the tangled underbrush, a figure lurked, her shape hunching low to the ground as though she were more beast than human. She was wrapped in dark, ragged layers that seemed to blend with the shadows around her. Her head was tilted downward, long strands of hair falling like a curtain across her face, matted and gray-streaked with age. The tattered cloth that clung to her thin frame swayed with an eerie, unnatural rhythm, and she muttered something unintelligible, her voice a low hiss that was both unsettling and strangely melodic.

As Wakamono and Red Mist drew closer, the figure slowly turned her head, revealing a hideous, distorted face. Her skin was an unnatural shade of blue-gray, stretched tight over sharp cheekbones, and her sunken, yellow eyes gleamed with a cruel intelligence. Her lips, twisted into a mocking sneer, revealed jagged teeth that seemed too sharp for any human mouth.

A kijo. There was no doubt about it.

Her gaze settled on Wakamono, and her eyes narrowed with an unnatural hunger. She took a step forward, her bare, clawed feet crunching over the dry, twisted leaves underfoot, and a chilling, mocking smile crept over her face.

"Well, well," she rasped, her voice like nails scraping over stone. "What brings such... fresh, young meat to my grove?"

Wakamono's grip on his blade tightened, and he fought to keep his breathing steady, but he felt her gaze prickle over his skin like venom. Beside him, Red Mist took a half-step forward, her expression unreadable, but her stance spoke of readiness, her body poised to strike at the first hint of an attack.

The kijo chuckled, a sound that grated against their nerves. "Oh, don't be so shy," she cooed, her eyes flicking between them with twisted delight. "Come closer."

Wakamono's pulse pounded in his ears as he took in her words and her mocking tone. He glanced at Red Mist, who held his gaze for a moment, offering a silent reminder of their purpose. There would be no retreat. Not from this.

The kijo's laughter faded into a chilling silence as she took another step forward, her form seeming to blend in and out of her surroundings, shadows clinging to her like a second skin. Her eyes, hollow and gleaming, focused intently on Wakamono, assessing him with a dark curiosity that made his skin crawl. Her long, skeletal fingers flexed, claws glinting in the dim light as if testing the air between them.

Wakamono steadied his stance, his grip firm, meeting her gaze without flinching. He could feel the weight of Red Mist's presence beside him, her calm anchoring him in place. The kijo's stare was unsettling, but Wakamono held his ground, resisting the urge to step back.

In an instant, the kijo's body contorted, her back arching in a series of unnatural movements that twisted her limbs at impossible angles. She moved with a disturbing fluidity, as though her bones were made of smoke. Her arms extended, fingers stretching to unnatural lengths, and her ragged robes fanned out around her like the tattered wings of a monstrous bird. The air thickened with a pungent, metallic scent, as if the forest itself recoiled from her.

Without warning, she lunged at them, her claws slicing through the air with a high-pitched whistle.

Wakamono ducked, narrowly dodging the razor-like claws that would have torn into him. Red Mist was already moving, her katana flashing as she countered the kijo's attack, her blade meeting the demon's claw with a clash that sent sparks into the shadows.

The kijo shrieked, an unholy sound that reverberated through the trees. She recoiled, but only for a moment before launching herself back at them, her twisted body bending and twisting in ways that defied natural movement. Wakamono raised his blade, instinct guiding his hand as he struck at her outstretched arm, managing to slice across her forearm. Dark, viscous blood oozed from the wound, and the kijo hissed in fury, retreating with a glare that promised retribution.

"Foolish child!" she snarled, her voice dripping with venom. "Do you think your feeble blade can deter me?"

Wakamono didn't respond, focusing instead on his breathing, steadying his stance. The kijo's gaze flicked to Red Mist, her lips curling into a sneer.

"And you..." she whispered, her voice low and taunting. "You carry the blood of a warrior, but I see something else in your eyes... doubt, perhaps? Fear?"

Red Mist's face remained impassive, but Wakamono could sense her resolve sharpening, her focus intensifying. She took a slow step forward, her katana raised, the blade gleaming with deadly intent.

"If you're hoping for fear, you'll be disappointed," Red Mist said calmly, her voice cold and unwavering. "But you'll find your end here, demon."

With a shriek, the kijo sprang forward again, her claws arcing toward them in a frenzy of motion. Wakamono moved instinctively, parrying her strikes, his blade slicing through the air as he kept pace with her erratic attacks. Red Mist advanced with calculated precision, each strike of her katana deliberate and controlled, forcing the kijo to retreat step by step.

The kijo staggered, her twisted form beginning to falter under the relentless onslaught of their combined attack. Her taunts dissolved into frenzied hisses as she fought back, her claws lashing out wildly, but her movements had grown slower, more desperate.

The kijo let out a piercing cry as Red Mist's blade slashed across her arm. Stumbling back, she glared at her opponents, fury and cunning gleaming in her yellow eyes.

The kijo's thin, crooked fingers traced a pattern through the air, her words twisting into the mist like threads weaving a dark spell. A thick, swirling fog rose from the ground, clouding Wakamono and Red Mist's vision, darkening the forest around them. Shadows flickered in the haze, the air filled with a chill that crept over Wakamono's skin, making him shiver.

As the fog grew dense, Wakamono's surroundings began to shift. The shapes in the mist twisted and transformed, forming ghostly figures that seemed all too real. His heart hammered in his chest as he watched his father's figure emerge from the fog, a towering, spectral vision in full battle regalia. His father's face was stern, eyes narrowing in disapproval. He took a step closer, his oversized katana glinting dangerously in the half-light.

"Failure," the apparition murmured, lifting the blade as if to strike.

Wakamono took a step back, but the fog around him thickened, and Hokori's face appeared, filled with bitter accusation. His brother's lips moved, though no sound escaped them, his eyes silently condemning Wakamono for the dangers brought upon their family. Then Bi materialized, her face a mask of sorrow, fragile and grieving. Her figure collapsed as a dark, monstrous hand lashed out from the fog and struck her down.

"Stop!" Wakamono shouted, slashing his blade through the apparitions, but they vanished, reforming elsewhere in the haze as if his strikes had no effect. He caught sight of other shapes—Shiro's face, twisted into a mocking grin, and familiar beasts he'd once fought, now lunging at him. He braced himself, his training pushing him to defend, but the creatures struck through his defenses, their forms ghostly and untouchable.

A voice cut through his rising panic, sharp and grounded. "They're illusions, Wakamono! Focus on what's real." Red Mist's tone was calm but strained, a rare note of tension slipping into her words. "Look past it—separate what you see from what you feel."

Her voice grounded him, pulling him from his fear. Wakamono's breathing slowed, his grip steadying on his blade. Red Mist, he realized, was caught in her own visions. He could see her steel herself, her eyes hardened as though facing some unseen threat. Yet despite the evil spirit's relentless tricks, she remained grounded, her focus unbreakable. Her words echoed in his mind as he centered himself, forcing his senses to quiet.

A soft, mocking laugh drifted through the fog. The kijo's voice seemed to come from every direction, taunting and sinister. "Oh, little Kōken," she sneered, her words stretching out like the fog itself. "You think you're safe? Beware—there is danger in the shadows."

Before he could react, he felt a sharp sting along his side—a thin line of pain as something slashed through his robes. Red Mist gave a quick, pained intake of breath as the kijo's claws raked across her arm. Waka-mono's hand went to his wound, feeling the warmth of his blood. The pain was real, grounding him, cutting through the illusions like a wake-up call.

Red Mist's gaze met his, fierce and steady. "Focus on the tangible," she murmured, low enough that only he could hear. "Feel the air, listen for the movements that are real. Look past the lies."

The visions continued to swirl around him, his father's condemning gaze, Hokori's bitterness, Bi's collapse, but Wakamono forced his mind to clear. He shifted his attention to the real, feeling the subtle disturbances in the air, the faint rustling of fabric that betrayed the kijo's movements. There—in the corner of his vision, a shadow moved with too much weight, too much substance.

He saw her. The kijo's wild, malevolent eyes, her claws outstretched for another strike, her form cloaked in the mist.

"Now," Red Mist whispered, her blade poised. In perfect unison, they lunged forward, their blades slicing through the air. The kijo let out a brief, guttural sound as their blades struck true, cutting through her twisted form.

The fog dissipated in an instant, replaced by a cloud of dark, swirling smoke. The kijo's form faded, her figure evaporating into darkness, leaving the corrupted forest silent and still.

Wakamono and Red Mist stood together in the quiet, catching their breath as the remnants of the kijo's illusions faded, leaving them alone in the twisted, haunted woods.

15
十五

THE FOREST HAD GONE unnaturally quiet. No birds sang, no leaves rustled in the cool autumn air. Even the distant hum of insects, ever-present in Seken's wilderness, had been swallowed by the oppressive silence. The trees, once strong and familiar, now loomed like skeletal sentinels, their twisted branches clawing toward the dim, unfeeling sky.

Red Mist slowed her pace, her katana resting at her side but ready, her hand firm on the hilt. Her eyes swept their surroundings, scanning every shadow and bend of the trees. She was never one to let emotions betray her, but the slight narrowing of her gaze spoke volumes. "Something's wrong," she murmured, more to herself than to Wakamono.

Wakamono, trailing just behind her, felt the weight of the air grow heavier with every step. The familiar ache of his burns from Onkai's grip flared faintly, as if his body was warning him of the unseen threat ahead. His hand tightened instinctively on his blade, his knuckles pale against the hilt. "This isn't like anything I've seen before," he said, his voice hushed. "It feels... alive and dead at the same time."

Red Mist's steps faltered, only for a fraction of a moment, before she pressed on. "Whatever it is, is it aware..." Her words trailed off as she reached out to touch the bark of a nearby tree. Her fingers barely brushed the surface before she pulled back sharply, her expression hardening.

"What is it?" Wakamono asked.

"The bark is warm," she replied, her voice clipped. "Like it's coursing with blood."

Wakamono shivered, his gaze darting to the dense shadows ahead. The low hum, which had started as barely perceptible, now vibrated in his chest, like the slow beat of a giant heart. "Do you think it's watching us?" he asked.

Red Mist didn't answer immediately. Her silence stretched, her gaze fixed on the warped forest ahead. "I don't know," she admitted finally, her tone low and steady. "More like feeling us; like it's waiting."

The hum deepened, and for a moment, the ground seemed to tremble beneath their feet. Wakamono stopped, his heart pounding. "Why it doing this?"

Red Mist turned to him, her sharp eyes locking onto his. "I don't think we'll like the answer."

The path ahead narrowed, the trees pressing in on either side as if to force them onward. Thorny vines hung like nooses from branches above, swaying in an unseen breeze. Red Mist's hand tightened on her katana. "Stay sharp. Whatever this is, it's pulling us toward it."

"You think it's leading us somewhere?" Wakamono asked.

Red Mist's lips pressed into a thin line. "No. Not somewhere. To something."

The weight of her words settled over Wakamono like the pressing air. He glanced back at the way they had come, the path now barely visible through the haze of fog and shadows. There was no turning back—not now. Taking a deep breath, he squared his shoulders and moved to walk beside Red Mist.

As they pressed forward, the hum grew louder, the forest itself seeming to tighten around them. The air was thick with decay, the scent of rotting wood and stagnant water clinging to their every breath. For a fleeting moment, Wakamono thought he saw something shift in the shadows—a dark, sinewy figure slithering just beyond his vision. He blinked, but it was gone.

The two Kōken marched on, side by side, toward the heart of the corruption.

後見

The oppressive hum had grown louder, reverberating through the forest like a pulse. The air itself felt thick and heavy, clinging to their skin as if the forest sought to entangle them. Red Mist and Wakamono pressed forward, their weapons drawn, their senses sharp. Every step was a struggle now, the ground beneath their feet soft and treacherous, like walking through a half-formed bog.

Ahead, the path twisted sharply, choked by a curtain of thorny vines. Red Mist slowed, holding up a hand to stop Wakamono. She studied the tangled growth, her brow furrowing as her gaze traced the unnatural angles of the vines. Their thorns glistened like shards of black glass, and they seemed to shift ever so slightly, as if alive.

"Careful," she said, her voice low. "These aren't ordinary brambles."

Before Wakamono could respond, the vines snapped forward like striking serpents. Red Mist moved instinctively, her katana slicing through the first wave with a clean, fluid motion. The severed vines writhed on the ground before curling inward and instantly rotting.

"Stay close," she commanded, her tone sharp but steady.

Wakamono nodded, gripping his blade tightly. The vines came at them in waves, lashing out from every direction. Wakamono swung his sword in quick, deliberate strikes, each movement precise. Despite his growing skill, he couldn't match Red Mist's effortless precision. Her blade flashed through the air, cutting down the attacking vines with a grace that seemed almost otherworldly.

"They're everywhere!" Wakamono shouted, ducking as a particularly thick vine swiped at his head. He spun around, slicing through it, but more took its place, slithering out from the trees like tentacles.

"They're driving us," Red Mist said, her voice tense but calm. "Not trying to kill us, just pushing us forward."

Wakamono's chest tightened at her words, and he spared a glance over his shoulder. The path behind them was completely blocked now, a dense wall of vines and brambles sealing off any chance of retreat. "Then we go forward," he said, determination hardening his voice.

As they pushed ahead, the vines became more aggressive, their movements faster and more coordinated. Wakamono gritted his teeth as a thorn sliced across his forearm, drawing blood. He swung his blade in retaliation, severing the vine and stepping closer to Red Mist.

The trees themselves seemed to lean in now, their gnarled branches anchoring violent vines. The hum grew louder, vibrating through the air and into their very bones. The ground beneath them became uneven, thick roots jutting up like traps waiting to ensnare them.

Suddenly, the ground shifted, and Wakamono stumbled. He caught himself just as a massive root shot up from the earth, narrowly missing his leg. He slashed at it, but his blade barely grazed the tough bark. Red Mist stepped in, her katana slicing cleanly through the root, leaving a faint, fading glow where it had been severed.

"We're almost there," she said, her eyes fixed ahead. "The corruption's at its peak."

The forest seemed to recoil at her words, as if acknowledging her challenge. The hum deepened, the vibrations now shaking the very ground they stood on. From the shadows ahead came the low, droning voice of the unseen enemy, each word resonating with an unnatural weight.

"Bring me the blade..."

Wakamono froze, his heart pounding. The voice didn't come from any single direction—it was everywhere, surrounding them, invading their minds. He looked to Red Mist, who stood firm, her katana at the ready.

"Forward," she said, her voice unwavering.

Wakamono nodded, gripping his blade tighter. Together, they pressed on, stepping deeper into the heart of the forest. The vines and roots lashed out more fiercely now, as if to weaken them prior to reaching their destination. But the Kōken moved with purpose, cutting through every obstacle in their path.

The air grew colder, the darkness more suffocating, as they neared the source of the land's vile transformation. Each step felt heavier, the weight of an ominous presence bearing down on them.

And still, the voice echoed: "Bring me the blade..."

The forest was alive with hostility. Wakamono's grip on his blade tightened as the air thickened around them, the rancid odors of death and decay invading his nostrils. Shadows stretched unnaturally, clawing at their path. The ground beneath their feet felt unstable, as if the very earth was shifting to impede them. The low, resonant hum that had been faint before now pressed against their senses, vibrating deep in their bones.

A sudden crack shattered the oppressive silence. From the underbrush, a massive boar emerged, its tusks glinting with a yellow, unnatural sheen. Its skin hung in patches, revealing raw muscle beneath, and a foul stench wafted toward them.

Wakamono tensed, his instincts kicking in. The boar charged, its glowing eyes locked onto him. He dodged to the side, but the beast twisted with a disturbing agility, raking its tusks against his blade.

The clash rattled up his arms. "This thing is strong!" he shouted, stepping back to regain his footing.

"Stay focused," Red Mist commanded, her voice cutting through the chaos. Her katana flashed, catching a vine creeping toward her legs. The severed tendril recoiled like a wounded snake, releasing a sickening hiss.

The boar charged again, its guttural roar reverberating through the clearing. Wakamono braced himself, blade ready, but before it could reach him, Red Mist's katana struck. The beast let out an unearthly shriek as her blade sliced clean through its side. It collapsed in a heap, black ichor spilling onto the corrupted soil. The creature struggled to rise and stumbled toward Wakamono before collapsing, motionless.

"That's one," Red Mist said curtly, her eyes scanning the forest for more threats. "Expect more."

As if summoned by the boar's death, a flock of mangled birds descended. Their feathers were sparse, their wings tattered, and their eyes burned with malice. They didn't squawk or caw but emitted an eerie, high-pitched drone, as if their vocal cords were in various states of decay.

"They're coming for us!" Wakamono warned, slashing at the first wave. His blade connected, and a bird exploded into a shower of feathers and viscous black fluid. But with each strike, the air filled with a choking haze of noxious spores.

Red Mist moved with precision, her strikes swift and deliberate. "Don't breathe it in!" she called, lifting a cloth over her nose and mouth. Wakamono followed suit, his lungs already burning from the tainted air.

They continued to thin the flock of diving foul, cutting through the mangy beasts with swift precision, until they retreated into the dense vines.

The hum deepened. The vibrations became almost unbearable, and then, the voice came.

"Bring me the blade."

Wakamono froze. The words still didn't seem to come from a single source but resonated from the trees, the ground, even the air. He looked to Red Mist, her expression hard and focused.

"Did you hear that?" he asked, his voice hoarse from breathing in the noxious air.

She nodded, her eyes scanning their surroundings. "We're close. And it's driving us toward it."

Before Wakamono could respond, the forest erupted again. Thorny vines lashed out, thick and sinewy, either trying to ensnare them or whip them into motion. The ground beneath their feet softened into a quagmire, threatening to swallow them whole. Wakamono slashed at a vine reaching for his leg, his blade cutting cleanly through, but more took its place.

The corrupted forest was relentless. Deer with jagged antlers and glowing red eyes charged from the shadows, and more birds dove toward them, their shrieks blending with the omnipresent hum. The noise and chaos were overwhelming.

"Move forward!" Red Mist ordered, her voice rising above the din. She cut through a tangle of vines with a single sweep of her katana. "It's driving us some-where, and we need to get there before it tears us apart!"

Wakamono didn't hesitate. They pushed forward, step by grueling step, cutting down anything in their path. The vines writhed, the ground shook and groaned, and the creatures kept coming, but Red Mist's mastery and Wakamono's growing skill kept them alive.

"Keep your focus," Red Mist said sharply as Waka-mono stumbled over a root. "We don't stop until we find the source."

The voice came again, more insistent this time. "Bring me the blade."

Wakamono's grip tightened on the hilt of his sword. "Then come and take it," he muttered under his breath, steeling himself as they pressed on into the corrupted heart of the forest.

The forest shuddered as Wakamono and Red Mist pressed on, their footsteps crunching through the withered foliage. The dense canopy above gave way to a gaping void of open sky, though the light seemed no brighter. A foreboding, unnatural silence replaced the cacophony of corrupted creatures that had hounded them moments before.

Red Mist slowed, her grip tightening on her katana. "Do you feel that?" she murmured, her voice low and cautious.

Wakamono nodded, his breath steady but his pulse quickening. The ground beneath their feet felt alive, vibrating faintly as if resonating with a heartbeat too large to comprehend. The trees at the forest's edge bent inward unnaturally, their gnarled branches twisting like claws, forming a jagged frame around the clearing.

As they stepped into the open, the air grew heavier, the clouded sky barely letting through more light than the canopy of the forest had. Wakamono's eyes scanned the expanse ahead—a vast clearing littered with the remnants of the forest's corruption. Dead animals and mangled plants lay scattered like offerings, their forms grotesquely warped. The sky above seemed darker than it should have been, as though the corruption reached even the heavens.

Red Mist's breath caught, a rare flicker of emotion crossing her face. Wakamono froze. There, in the center of the clearing, was the source of the corruption—the force that had twisted the forest and sent creatures to their doom.

It loomed, its shifting, sinewy form barely discernible through the gloom, a nightmare given shape. The hum deepened, rattling their bones and making the air itself seem to pulse with dread.

And then, as if sensing their presence, the shadowed mass began to shift. A tremor rippled through the ground, and the clearing seemed to recoil in antic-

ipation. Slowly, impossibly, it moved—its form undu-
lating with an eerie, primal rhythm that defied nature
itself. Every appendage and tendril seemed to shift
toward them, a harbinger of something ancient and
malevolent awakening to their intrusion.

16 十五

THE TOWERING FORM OF the akuma loomed over Wakamono and Red Mist. Its tendrils, grotesque and rugged, writhed out from its abdomen like living serpents, reaching and recoiling as though testing the air for its prey. Each movement sent ripples through the ground, and the low, resonant hum emanating from the void where its face should have been grew louder, vibrating in their chests.

Wakamono gripped his blade tightly, the weight of its hilt grounding him as he prepared for the next attack. Red Mist shifted her stance, her katana gleaming in the dim, corrupted light.

Without warning, a cluster of tendrils lashed out from the beast. Wakamono ducked just in time, the air whipping above his head as the tentacle-like arms thrust into the ground behind him. Red Mist seized the moment, her blade slicing cleanly through one of the writhing appendages. Instead of falling limp, the severed piece twitched violently and slithered back toward the akuma, disappearing into its twisted frame with a sickening squelch.

The creature paused briefly, almost as if assessing, before a new wave of tendrils erupted from its abdomen. They slammed into the ground, wrapping around massive rocks like iron chains. With an almost casual motion, the akuma lifted one into the air and hurled it forward.

The rock hurtled toward them, the sheer force splitting the ground as it struck. Wakamono leapt to the side, rolling to avoid the debris, while Red Mist darted forward, her katana slashing at the incoming tendrils.

Another boulder came crashing down, shaking the earth and sending shards of stone flying. The sheer power of the akuma's attack sent a sharp pang of doubt through Wakamono, but he pushed it aside, focusing on the movements of the terrible form.

"Keep moving!" Red Mist commanded, her voice cutting through the chaos.

Wakamono nodded, dodging another tendril that whipped dangerously close to his face. He swung his blade in a wide arc, cutting into one of the tendrils. This time, it retracted sharply, spraying a thick, tar-like substance that hissed as it hit the ground.

Red Mist darted forward, her movements precise and deadly, as she landed a blow that sliced cleanly into the creature's side. The akuma let out a deep, resonant groan, the sound echoing through the clearing. It twisted its body, dragging its tendrils through the earth, uprooting trees and sending a wall of dirt and debris toward its attackers.

The onslaught intensified. Wakamono and Red Mist fought side by side, their strikes coordinated yet desperate. The akuma's tendrils seemed endless, each one lashing out with relentless precision. For every appendage they severed, another took its place, recoiling and reforming with an unnatural fluidity.

Wakamono's breath came in ragged gasps as he deflected another strike. He glanced toward Red Mist, whose bladework remained sharp and deliberate despite the chaos. The ground beneath them trembled, as if the forest itself were alive and angry, the akuma's power reaching its zenith.

"Stay focused," Red Mist said sharply, her voice a grounding force amidst the storm whipping tendrils and flying debris.

Wakamono steadied himself, gripping his blade tighter as he prepared for the next wave. The creature's head seemed to tilt toward them, its low hum vibrating with an almost mocking intensity. It was toying with them, and the realization only steeled Wakamono's resolve.

As the tendrils lashed out once more, Wakamono and Red Mist moved in tandem, their blades cutting through the corruption. But the akuma showed no signs of weakening, its monstrous form seeming to grow larger and more menacing as the battle raged on.

And then, with a deliberate slowness, it raised another massive rock, its tendrils curling tightly around it. The sound of cracking stone echoed through the clearing, a harbinger of the chaos yet to come.

The forest's dense corruption seemed to draw tighter around Wakamono and Red Mist, each shadow heavier, each step harder to take. The tendrils that writhed from the akuma's abdomen moved with unnatural precision, their jagged ends curling around rocks and ground alike, pulling the hulking form of the creature forward like a grotesque puppet master.

Wakamono's eyes narrowed. He remembered the healing blade. The memory of Onkai flashed through his mind—the way the blade had pierced through the akuma's hardened shell, exposing a vulnerability that had allowed their eventual victory. This had to work again. It had to.

Red Mist, her katana raised in readiness, didn't speak. She didn't need to. Her steady presence beside him was grounding, even as the air thrummed with the low, vibrating hum emanating from the creature.

Wakamono darted forward, his movement swift and deliberate. Hanron's tendrils whipped toward him, one narrowly grazing his shoulder as he sidestepped and rolled beneath another. His katana flashed, severing an incoming tendril, though the demon seemed undeterred.

The hum grew louder.

Wakamono gritted his teeth. This was his chance. He surged closer, his training taking over as he dodged the relentless strikes. Red Mist drew their attention away momentarily, slashing through the brambles that clawed toward her. Her movements were fluid, her strikes precise, but it was clear the akuma's focus was on Wakamono—and the blade.

With a cry, Wakamono lunged, pulling the healing blade from his pack and thrusting it deep into Hanron's torso. The force of the strike reverberated up his arms, and for a brief moment, he thought he'd done it. The akuma stilled, its tendrils pausing mid-snap.

But instead of recoiling or crying out in pain, the creature's tendrils slowly curled around the blade's hilt, pulling it deeper into itself. A low, guttural laugh rumbled from the void where its face should have been. The laugh vibrated in the air, resonating with an eerie sense of triumph.

"What—" Wakamono stumbled back, his chest heaving as he watched the creature straighten, its sinewy form somehow more menacing. The blade, buried within its pale, shifting torso, pulsed faintly, its power now serving the creature's twisted purpose.

Red Mist moved to his side, her katana raised defensively. "Wakamono, stay sharp!" she barked, her tone edged with alarm but still steady.

Wakamono barely had time to respond before the creature surged forward, its movements faster and more deliberate than before. Red Mist intercepted a tendril with her blade, slicing cleanly through it—but the wound sealed itself almost instantly, the tendril regenerating with alarming speed.

"It's healing," Wakamono said, his voice tight with disbelief. "The blade—it's making it stronger."

Red Mist's gaze darted between the creature and the healing blade embedded in its torso. Her lips pressed into a grim line. "Then we don't stop. We just strike faster, harder."

The creature lunged again, its massive tendrils sweeping low. Wakamono and Red Mist moved in unison, their strikes a flurry of steel. They worked together seamlessly, each attack aimed to exploit the openings left by the other, but no matter how precise or fierce their blows, the akuma continued to regenerate.

The forest seemed to close in around them, the corrupted ground twisting underfoot as the hum grew louder, a maddening drone that seemed to press against their very thoughts. For every strike they landed, the akuma countered with its relentless tendrils, its body unyielding and ever-shifting.

Wakamono's breath came in ragged gasps as he blocked another strike, his blade flashing upward to sever an attacking tendril. "Red Mist, it's—"

"I know!" she cut him off, her voice sharp. "Stay focused!"

The battle raged on, their strikes desperate, the creature's regeneration relentless. The air was heavy with the tension of a fight they weren't winning. And all the while, the hum deepened, vibrating in their bones, as if the akuma's presence alone was enough to break them.

Finally, Red Mist and Wakamono broke apart, standing side by side as the creature loomed before them, its form unscathed despite the ferocity of their attacks. Wakamono tightened his grip on his blade, his muscles trembling with exhaustion.

"It's stronger than anything we've faced," he said, his voice barely above a whisper.

Red Mist didn't reply. Her gaze remained fixed on the akuma, her stance resolute. The battle wasn't over yet—but the odds were turning grim.

The forest seemed alive in its malevolence. Vines lashed out like serpents, twisting through the air with predatory precision. Trees groaned, their skeletal branches bending and weaving into barriers that blocked any retreat. Thick roots erupted from the ground, clawing at the feet of Wakamono and Red Mist as if the very ground sought to drag them under.

Red Mist, her movements sharp but visibly strained, cut through the barrage of vines with her katana. Each strike was perfectly placed, but the endless waves of attacks were taking their toll. Her shoulders heaved as she spun and sliced, the glint of her blade barely keeping the relentless onslaught at bay.

"Don't give up!" she shouted over her shoulder, her voice edged with tension.

Wakamono barely heard her. He was too busy dodging the writhing roots that tore through the ground beneath him. One vine snapped toward his face, and he ducked just in time, feeling the rush of air as it missed him by inches. The attacks came faster, closer to succeeding. His focus wavered for a split second as he glanced toward Red Mist.

She was forced back by the akuma's tendrils, her strikes meeting resistance with each swing. The healing blade embedded in its torso pulsed faintly, and with each pulse, the akuma grew bolder, stronger. Its tendrils slashed out in all directions, tearing through the corrupted surroundings with terrifying speed.

The hum emanating from the creature had grown louder, deeper, vibrating through Wakamono's chest. It felt as though the sound itself was pressing down on him, a weight that threatened to crush his resolve. Doubt crept in, sharp and unwelcome.

We can't win this. It's too strong. The thought struck him like a blow, his hand tightening on the hilt of his katana. For a moment, he faltered, his movements slowing as the enormity of the akuma's power loomed over him.

A sharp cry brought him back. Red Mist had been thrown against a gnarled tree by one of the akuma's tendrils, her katana pinned beneath a writhing vine. She struggled to free it, her teeth clenched in frustration. The akuma moved toward her, its sickly tendrils coiling like snakes, ready to strike.

"No!" Wakamono shouted, forcing his battered body forward. His legs burned with exhaustion, and his side throbbed where a vine had struck him earlier, but he pressed on, his katana slicing through the corrupted growths that tried to block his path.

A massive tendril lashed out, catching him in the chest and sending him sprawling to the ground. His katana skittered away, just out of reach. Gasping for air, Wakamono tried to crawl toward it, his fingers clawing at the dirt, but the tendrils were faster. One coiled tightly around his leg, dragging him back.

The akuma loomed over Red Mist, its grotesque form towering against the darkened forest edge. The healing blade pulsed within its torso, and its guttural hum grew into a laugh—low, resonant, and filled with triumph. Its tendrils raised high, poised to strike.

"Red Mist!" Wakamono's voice cracked as he reached out, helplessly watching as the scene unfolded. His katana lay just beyond his fingertips, the edge glinting faintly in the dim light, weak and useless on the ground, just as Wakamono was himself.

十五

THE BATTLEFIELD ROARED WITH chaos as Wakamono and Red Mist struggled to hold their ground.
The akuma, now surging with unnatural strength,
lashed out with relentless precision. Amid the cacophony, a figure stepped quietly into the clearing,
unnoticed by either combatant or beast.

Kaida moved with deliberate calm, his staff tap-
ping softly against the ground. His weathered robes
brushed the undergrowth, untouched by the remnants
of corruption that clung to the environment. The hum
of the akuma's presence reverberated through the air,
but Kaida seemed unaffected, as though he walked in
a sphere of tranquility.

The old seer paused, his gaze sweeping over the
scene. His eyes, sharp and discerning despite his
years, locked onto the center of the chaos—the twisting form of the akuma. Kaida's expression betrayed no
surprise, no fear, only a quiet resolve.

Dropping to his knees and lowering his staff to the ground in front of him, Kaida murmured to himself, "Hanron, your corruption ends now."

Kaida leaned forward, resting both hands atop his staff. His voice, low and steady, began to weave an incantation. Though barely above a whisper, the words carried an unnatural weight, resonating through the corrupted air like ripples in a still pond.

Kaida leaned on his staff, his soft voice carrying his intent like a breeze parting dense fog:

"Roots break tainted soil,
Light conquers the ancient dark—
Shadows fall to dust."

A faint shimmer surrounded him, subtle at first, but growing into a translucent barrier that pulsed with his breath. The energy radiated outward, faint ripples that bent the mist around him. Kaida's presence, though unassuming, began to disrupt the oppressive aura of the clearing.

Hanron froze mid-swipe, one of its sinewy tendrils poised to strike Red Mist. Its faceless head tilted toward the intruder, the low hum intensifying, vibrating through the air like a predator's growl.

Kaida did not flinch.

The akuma, enraged, redirected its full focus toward the old seer. Its tendrils lashed out, each movement filled with lethal intent. But as they neared

Kaida's barrier, the strikes deflected harmlessly, the energy shimmering with each impact.

"Old relic," Hanron's voice vibrated through the air, guttural and mocking. "Do you believe simple words can unmake me?"

Kaida's gaze remained serene. "Your strength lies in darkness, twisted roots and stolen life. You have overstepped, Hanron."

Wakamono, still trying to rise, heard the name spoken aloud for the first time. "Hanron..." he murmured, the name carving itself into his memory like a warning etched in stone.

Hanron's tendrils recoiled momentarily, but only to gather force. They struck the barrier with renewed vigor, the clearing trembling under the repeated impacts. Yet Kaida's staff remained planted, his voice steady as he repeated, each word laced with unyielding resolve:

"Roots break tainted soil,
Light conquers the ancient dark—
Shadows fall to dust."

The akuma snarled, its tendrils writhing furiously. It leaned its entire weight into the assault, but Kaida stayed resolute. His barrier held, shimmering brighter with each word he spoke.

Kaida's voice rose, echoing through the clearing like a mantra of defiance. Each repetition sent a ripple of energy through the ground, fracturing the earth beneath Hanron, putting to rest the corruption around him. The akuma bellowed, its tendrils slamming against the barrier with unrelenting force, but they now recoiled as if burned. The hum that emanated from its faceless void grew erratic, its once overbearing resonance faltering under Kaida's words.

With a final, guttural snarl, Hanron reared back, drawing upon its full strength. Its tendrils thickened, coiling together to form a massive limb that it swung toward Kaida with deadly intent. The ground quaked under the force of the strike.

Kaida braced himself, leaning into his staff. "Roots break tainted soil..." His voice remained calm, unwavering, as the massive limb collided with his barrier, smashing the protective sphere and all it contained several inches into the ground. The air shimmered violently, the impact sending shockwaves through the clearing. Dust and debris filled the air, obscuring the scene.

For a moment, silence reigned.

Then, the dust began to settle, revealing Kaida unwavering, his barrier intact though visibly weakened. He took a labored breath, sweat dripping from his brow, but his resolve was unshaken.

Hanron writhed in fury, its tendrils lashing out blindly as it recoiled. The ground beneath it cracked and shifted, blackened roots curling inward as if retreating from Kaida's presence, embracing death, their release from Hanron's thrall.

Kaida lifted his staff and slammed it into the earth. "Light conquers the ancient dark—shadows fall to dust!" His voice resonated with a force that seemed to come from the earth itself.

A wave of energy burst forth, spreading outward in concentric circles. The corrupted plants and animals nearest to Hanron continued to wither, their twisted forms collapsing into decay. The vines clutching at Wakamono and Red Mist fell limp, releasing their hold.

The akuma staggered, its tendrils quivering as the wave reached it. Though it resisted, cracks began to form along its rough skin. Hanron roared, a guttural sound that shook the clearing, but its strength was clearly waning.

Wakamono, now free, scrambled to his feet and rushed to Red Mist's side. She was badly bruised but alive, already pushing herself up. They exchanged a look, their silent understanding clear: Kaida had shifted the tide of the battle, but it was far from over.

Kaida, however, was beginning to falter. His breaths came faster, each one more labored than the last. The glow of his barrier flickered, and the tremor in his hands betrayed the toll the fight was taking on him. Yet his voice never wavered as he continued, repeating the words with a steadfast determination.

"Roots break tainted soil,
Light conquers the ancient dark—
Shadows fall to dust."

The clearing trembled under the combined forces of Kaida's determination and Hanron's desperate fury. The akuma, though weakened, was relentless, lashing out with its massive tendrils. The healing blade embedded in its torso pulsed faintly, as if resisting the now weakened corruption that surrounded it.

Kaida's voice carried on, though strained. "Shadows fall to dust..." Each syllable was like a hammer blow, sending shockwaves through the ground. His barrier, however, was visibly cracking, the once radiant energy now dim and uneven, pulsing wildly.

Hanron roared, its hum rising in pitch and intensity. The air vibrated with its anger, the sound rattling the bones of everyone present. With an ear-splitting screech, it continued to focus its tendrils on Kaida, launching them in a coordinated attack.

The old man flinched but held firm, raising his staff to reinforce the barrier. The tendrils slammed into the shimmering shield, splintering it like glass. Kaida groaned, but his voice didn't falter. He struck the ground with his staff, sending another wave of energy rippling outward.

"Shadows fall to dust!" The wave struck Hanron, forcing it to recoil. Cracks spidered across the akuma's writing form, its tendrils momentarily retreating.

Wakamono and Red Mist seized the opportunity. With synchronized precision, they launched themselves at Hanron. Wakamono struck at the akuma's vulnerable joints, aiming to sever its tendrils, while Red Mist delivered decisive, calculated blows to its core. The once-impervious creature now bled dark ichor from its wounds.

But Hanron was far from defeated. The akuma surged forward with a sudden burst of energy, sweeping its massive tendrils across the clearing. Wakamono and Red Mist were sent sprawling, the sheer force of the attack knocking the wind from their lungs. Hanron turned its attention back to Kaida, who remained kneeling, his staff trembling in his grip.

Kaida's voice was barely audible now, his strength waning. "Light conquers the ancient dark..." He repeated the line, his breath hitching as he fought to maintain the barrier. Hanron loomed over him, its towering form casting a shadow that seemed to devour the dim light of the clearing.

"Kaida!" Wakamono cried out, scrambling to his feet. But Red Mist grabbed his arm, shaking her head. "He knows what he's doing," she said, her voice heavy with the weight of understanding.

Kaida met Hanron's faceless gaze, his own eyes calm, resolute. "It ends," he said, not as a shout, but a simple, unwavering truth. Summoning the last of his strength, Kaida raised his staff high and slammed it into the ground.

The earth erupted with a blinding wave of energy, surging outward like a tidal wave. Hanron let out a deafening roar, its tendrils thrashing violently as the wave consumed it. The cracks along its body deepened, its outer layers peeling away, and with a final, guttural sound, the akuma collapsed, crumbling into a mound of blackened dirt and ash.

Kaida fell forward, catching himself weakly on his withered hands. The clearing was silent now, save for the faint rustling of leaves as the corruption began to recede. The twisted plants and animals surrounding them withered and fell away, leaving behind an eerie stillness.

Wakamono and Red Mist rushed to Kaida's side. The old man looked up at them, his face pale and gaunt but serene. His voice was barely above a whisper: "The young one... the blade... the balance..." His words trailed off, his strength finally giving out.

Kaida collapsed, his body limp. Red Mist closed her eyes, placing a hand over his chest. Wakamono clenched his fists, tears streaking his dirt-covered face as he looked at the man who had saved them, saved so many. Kaida's breathing became ragged.

The clearing was quiet, the air cool and crisp as the first rays of dawn broke through the trees. Hanron's presence was gone, and with it, the corruption that had plagued the forest. But the scars of the battle remained, a stark reminder of the cost of their victory.

The stillness, however, was short-lived.

From the shadows beyond the clearing, a figure emerged—a hunched, frail woman, her pale skin stretched tightly over sharp, angular bones. Her hair hung in tangled strands, and her elongated fingers dragged lightly against her sides as she stepped forward. Her eyes gleamed faintly, reflecting the dim light of the clearing.

"You weren't supposed to be here, old man," she whispered, her voice soft yet venomous. It slithered through the clearing, cutting through the relief like a blade. Her gaze was fixed on Kaida, and though her tone was calm, her words dripped with malice.

Kaida, unable to move from Red Mist's arms, didn't flinch. "You will fail, Yama-uba," he said simply, his voice steady despite his obvious weakness.

A thin, cruel smile curled across Yama-uba's lips. "Perhaps. Perhaps not. But you won't be around to see it," she murmured.

Before Wakamono or Red Mist could react, Yama-uba surged forward with inhuman speed. Her elongated fingers, tipped with razor-sharp nails, plunged into Kaida's back with a sickening sound. The old man stiffened, his body convulsing slightly as the ensured his demise.

"Kaida!" Wakamono shouted, his voice breaking. He tried to push himself to his feet, but his battered body refused to respond quickly enough.

Kaida turned his head slightly, just enough to glance over his shoulder at Yama-uba. Despite the blood trickling from his lips, his expression remained calm. "The light will find you, even in the dark," he said, his voice barely above a whisper.

Yama-uba sneered, twisting her nails before withdrawing them. Kaida collapsed fully, his staff rolling from his grip.

"Such faith," Yama-uba said, her voice mocking. "Such... foolishness."

As Wakamono and Red Mist surged forward, weapons ready, Yama-uba stepped back into the shadows, her body dissolving into the darkness. "Enjoy your hollow victory," her voice echoed, disembodied now. "Your luck... fleeting."

And then she was gone.

Wakamono dropped to his knees beside Kaida, his hands trembling as he reached out to the old man. "Kaida."

Red Mist stood silently, her katana held loosely at her side. Her lips pressed into a thin line, but the sorrow in her eyes betrayed her stoic mask.

Kaida's breathing was shallow, his life slipping away with each passing second. He looked up at Wakamono, a faint smile breaking through his pain.

"You... did well," he said, his voice faint but resolute. "Carry the light forward."

And with that, his eyes closed, his body going limp in Wakamono's arms.

From the remains of Hanron, Red Mist pulled the healing blade.

18 十五

THE CLEARING NEAR KAIDA'S cave was untouched by the corruption that had ravaged the forest nearby. The trees stood tall and steadfast, their leaves a vibrant tapestry of autumn reds and golds. A soft breeze carried the faint scent of pine, mingled with the earthy aroma of fallen leaves. The sunlight, filtered through the dense canopy above, dappled the ground with patches of warm light.

Red Mist and Wakamono stood at the edge of the clearing, both silent as they took in the tranquil scene. It was hard to believe that only days earlier, they had fought for their lives against a force of unimaginable malice. Here, it was as though the world had never known corruption or violence.

"This place..." Wakamono whispered, his voice hushed as if he feared breaking the stillness.

"It's untouched," Red Mist said, her tone even, though there was a hint of reverence in her voice. "A place of peace."

Wakamono looked toward the cave, its dark mouth blending seamlessly with the mountain. It felt strange, almost intrusive, to bring Kaida's body here, but he knew it was what the old man would have wanted. Kaida had lived here, connected to this land, and it was fitting that he would rest here as well.

As they approached the clearing's center, Wakamono couldn't shake the weight pressing on his chest. He glanced at the wrapped bundle they carried—Kaida's lifeless form, swaddled in the fabric of his own robes. The old man had walked into the heart of corruption and faced the impossible, all to ensure their survival.

Wakamono's grip on the stretcher tightened. "Do you think... he found peace?" he asked, his voice unsteady.

Red Mist glanced at him, her expression unreadable but her eyes softened. "Kaida lived his life with purpose. His peace was in his duty. That's more than most can claim."

Wakamono nodded, though the ache in his chest didn't ease. They reached the center of the clearing and set Kaida down gently, the stretcher resting on the soft grass. The clearing, serene as it was, seemed to hold its breath, waiting for what came next.

Wakamono crouched, running his hands over the ground. The soil was firm but workable, the kind of earth that seemed to welcome its role in Kaida's burial. Beside him, Red Mist knelt without hesitation and began to dig with her hands.

Wakamono followed her lead, scooping handfuls of dirt with quiet determination. The act was somber, almost meditative. Neither spoke, their shared silence a tribute to the man who had given everything for them.

As they dug, Wakamono's fingers caught on something sharp—a jagged rock buried in the soil. He winced, pulling his hand back to see a thin line of blood beading on his palm.

Red Mist noticed immediately. She reached over, tearing a strip of cloth from her sleeve and wrapping it around his hand with practiced efficiency. "A clean wound," she remarked. "It'll scar, but nothing worse."

Wakamono flexed his fingers, watching the red seep through the fabric. "Another scar to add to the collection," he muttered, his voice bitter.

Red Mist paused, her hands resting lightly on his. "Every scar is a story, Wakamono. This one will remind you of Kaida and his sacrifice. It's how we honor those who've fallen—by carrying their memory, even when it hurts."

Her words struck something deep within him. Wakamono looked at the shallow grave they were creating and felt the weight of her lesson settle over him. The sting in his hand seemed to fade as he nodded, determination returning to his eyes.

Together, they continued to dig, their movements steady and deliberate. The sun began to dip lower in the sky, casting long shadows across the clearing as they worked.

When the grave was ready, they both paused, gazing at the resting place they had prepared. It was simple, unadorned, yet fitting.

"Kaida deserved more," Wakamono said softly.

Red Mist straightened, her gaze fixed on the horizon. "Kaida deserved the peace he fought for. And now, he has it."

後見

As the last light of day filtered through the canopy, Red Mist and Wakamono stood side by side, facing the grave they had dug. Kaida's wrapped form lay at the edge of the pit, serene and still, his staff resting across his chest.

Red Mist stepped forward first, kneeling beside the grave. She placed her hands on Kaida's staff, bowing her head for a moment of silent reflection. The stillness was profound, the clearing itself seeming to honor the moment.

"Kaida lived as all Kōken should," she said, her voice calm but heavy with meaning. "With honor. With purpose. His life was not measured by how it ended, but by what he left behind." She paused, her gaze distant, as though recalling battles fought long before Wakamono's time. "We fight knowing our end is inevitable. But Kaida... he chose when and how his story would close. There's no greater strength than that."

Wakamono, standing behind her, clenched his fists at her words. He stepped forward, kneeling opposite Red Mist. His voice wavered as he spoke. "He was more than a Kōken. He saved us. Without him..." He trailed off, his throat tightening.

Red Mist looked across at him, her expression softening. "Without him, you wouldn't be here to carry on. And you will carry on, Wakamono. You must."

Together, they lowered Kaida into the grave, his body resting in the earth that had been his sanctuary. Wakamono's hands trembled as he reached for a handful of soil, scattering it over Kaida's body. Red Mist followed suit, her movements deliberate and steady.

For a moment, neither spoke. The sound of the soil falling into the grave filled the air, grounding them in the gravity of the moment.

後見

As the grave was filled, the final rays of sunlight gave way to twilight. Wakamono sat back, his gaze fixed on the small mound of earth that now marked Kaida's resting place.

Red Mist remained standing, her silhouette sharp against the fading light. She spoke, her voice low but firm. "Every Kōken walks this path knowing the price of their duty. Kaida accepted it without hesitation. And so will we."

Wakamono looked up at her, his expression conflicted. "But... does it always have to end like this?"

Red Mist turned her gaze to the grave, her eyes unreadable. "Every path has its end, Wakamono. What matters is how we walk it."

The weight of her words settled heavily over him. He glanced at the scar on his palm, now wrapped in the strip of cloth Red Mist had tied earlier. The wound would heal, but the memory would remain.

Red Mist stepped forward, her hand resting briefly on Wakamono's shoulder. "Rest now. Tomorrow, we go."

Wakamono nodded, his eyes lingering on the grave as Red Mist walked toward the edge of the clearing. The night was silent save for the faint rustle of leaves, the forest seeming to acknowledge the passing of one of its own.

For a long moment, Wakamono sat alone, the stars beginning to emerge above him. He whispered softly, his words carrying into the stillness. "Thank you, Kaida. I won't forget."

With that, he rose, following Red Mist as they for shelter. The faint silhouette of Kaida's resting place faded into the shadows of the night, a solemn reminder of the cost—and honor—of the path they had chosen.

END

終

EPILOGUE

THE AIR INSIDE THE cave was heavy, damp with a lingering sense of decay. A dark, shifting form loomed before Yama-uba, its presence filling the cavern. The remaining akuma was unlike its predecessors—its body wavered and twisted like thick, black smoke, vapor curling and unfurling as if tethered to the shadows themselves. It seemed almost incorporeal, but the oppressive weight of its presence was undeniable.

Yama-uba stood rigid, her frail figure somehow commanding, her aged face twisting into a mask of scorn. Her blackened nails tapped rhythmically against her wooden staff, the sound echoing faintly in the hollow chamber.

"Another failure," she hissed, her voice slicing through the silence. "Hanron fell, just as Onkai did. And you..." She pointed her staff at the smoke-like form. "Success? Or... dissipate like the weak embers you are?"

The akuma did not respond, its form swirling silently. It showed no fear, no anger. Its ghost-like figure seemed to absorb her words, processing them in an alien way that made Yama-uba's tone sharpen further.

"Do you think your silence protects you?" she spat, stepping closer. "You will serve... and not fail me. No choice."

The shadows within the cave seemed to quiver, and a deep, low pulse resonated from the farthest recesses of the cavern. The stone walls shimmered faintly, slick with an unseen, otherworldly ichor. The akuma remained motionless, the pulse of the cave reflecting faintly in its dark, shifting form.

Yama-uba tilted her head toward the depths of the cave, her sharp gaze narrowing as if listening to a distant whisper. For the first time, her scornful expression faltered, replaced by something closer to reverence—or unease.

"Patience," she murmured, her tone soft but still sharp with defiance. "Your hunger will be sated. Seken will kneel. But first...the blade."

The cave seemed to breathe, a low, guttural rumble building until it was almost deafening. Shadows stretched unnaturally across the chamber floor, converging on a single point—an abyss at the farthest end of the cavern. The air grew colder, vibrating with a palpable malevolence.

The akuma began to shift toward the abyss, drawn to its dark gravity. As it neared, its form became darker, more condensed, as if feeding off the abyss itself. Yama-uba stepped back, her grip on her staff tightening, her sharp eyes fixed on the darkness.

The rumbling subsided, leaving an eerie stillness in its wake. The shadows receded, but the oppressive energy remained, pressing against her chest like an invisible weight. She turned away sharply, muttering under her breath, "Even you will not rush me."

As she walked toward the mouth of the cave, the faint echoes of laughter followed her—not hers, but something deeper, more sinister, and filled with a terrible promise.

Outside, far below the steep mountainside, the corrupted forest had begun to heal, the twisted branches and blackened soil showing signs of young life. But the cave stood untouched, its dark presence festering like a wound in the heart of Seken.

www.ingramcontent.com/pod-product-compliance
Lightning Source LLC
Chambersburg PA
CBHW022121170626
46808CB00002B/803